Slaughtered in the Sand

WREN AND RASCAL COZY MYSTERY, BOOK 4

JUDITH A. BARRETT

WOBBLY CREEK, LLC

Dedication

Slaughtered in the Sand is dedicated to the color emerald green and to readers who love pirates.

Slaughtered in the Sand

Wren and Rascal Cozy Mystery, Book 4

Published in the United States of America by Wobbly Creek, LLC

2024 Georgia

wobblycreek.com

Cover by Wobbly Creek, LLC

ISBN 978-1-953870-58-2 eBook

ISBN 978-1-953870-59-9 Paperback

Previously

WREN

My name is Wren Weaver; I'm a freelance journalist and a camping enthusiast, so I was excited about the offer from a travel magazine publisher that combined my two passions. My assignment is to write about four haunted campgrounds across the United States and to provide feedback on the trailers we use for camping.

My constant companion is Rascal, my four-year-old black and tan Labrador Retriever, with a smidgeon of Husky. Our first assignment was at the Forgotten Oasis Campground in Hidden Gulch, Arizona; the second was in Dry Creek, Texas, and the third was in Dearheart, Tennessee.

Our camper was destroyed in a flood in Tennessee, so the publisher had to adjust his original plan for our fourth assignment because he said it was too far away for us to travel without a camper for our overnight accommodations. Rascal and I are on our way to Mobile, Alabama, to pick up our camper before we head to Lost Pirate Campground near Sirens Beach, Florida.

Rascal and I will return to Arizona after we complete our fourth haunted campground article. Even though we were in Hidden Gulch for only a week, Marshal Justin Lewis and I became more than just friends, and our relationship keeps growing stronger. Meanwhile, I miss him like crazy.

My publisher, Charlie Hogue, hired his nephew, Blake, my two-timing former boyfriend from college. After Blake twice repeated his old trick of trying to insert himself into my writing, Charlie realized I was serious when I told him to publish my articles or return them to me and give the assignment to Blake. Charlie published my third article without Blake's attempts to interfere.

When I was in college, I had very few friends because I was so focused on my studies; now I have good friends in Arizona, Texas, and Tennessee, including at least four ghosts.

JUSTIN

I'm Justin Lewis, the marshal at Hidden Gulch; after I lost my wife in a car crash three years ago, I threw myself into my work and forgot all about women, but then I met Wren. When she gazed at me with her emerald green eyes and spoke to me in her soft, Georgia accent, she melted my heart that I thought had frozen long ago. She's petite and looks fragile, but that green-eyed beauty with light brown hair and streaks of red that look like fire is absolutely fearless, and she terrifies me with the chances she takes.

She promised the Forgotten Oasis Campground ghost, Thomas, that she'd be back in six weeks, but we won't have to wait that long to see her after all because she is such a talented journalist that she has been completing each article in less than a week.

Wren and I are becoming closer every day in spite of the miles between us. I intend for her to come to Arizona and stay permanently. I think she agrees, but maybe I should take the next step to make sure it happens.

Chapter One

"You must be Wren Weaver and Rascal," the woman behind the service desk at the Mobile, Alabama, RV dealership said. "We were sorry to hear about your trailer being ruined in a flood, but we're glad to have you here. We got a call to check your hitch, but that won't take long."

While Wren examined the display of coffee mugs, she whispered, "I'll bet Justin called them."

Rascal grinned.

Wren sent a text to Justin. "At the RV place; they're checking my hitch because you called them."

He replied, "Good."

Wren smiled. *He didn't apologize or deny it.*

When Wren returned to the service desk, the woman said, "The campground will give you a flyer about our nearby restaurants that deliver. After a long day of driving, you might let someone else do the cooking and cleanup."

"Thanks. Do you have a favorite?"

"I'm partial to Cajun."

Wren smiled. "So am I."

A middle-aged man with the RV dealership logo on the chest pocket of his gray shirt came into the service office from a side door. His brow was furrowed. "Are you Wren Weaver?"

"Yes, sir."

The man exhaled as he approached her. "You probably know your bumper needs to be replaced, but your hitch was damaged too; it's not safe for your pickup to pull a trailer, but we've got an alternative for you while your truck is being repaired. It's ready to go; come see what you think."

When they went out the side door, Wren scanned the area but saw only trailers. She followed the service manager.

When he stopped at a van, he smiled. "What do you think?"

Wren stared at the vehicle.

"It has a pop-up roof; I understand you'll be camping near a beach," he said. "This is a perfect camper for a beach vacation on the Emerald Coast; you'll blend right in."

Wren crossed her arms and frowned. "It has a composting toilet, doesn't it?"

The man's smile disappeared. "Sorry. The CEO said you wouldn't be happy, but it was the best we could do. He said he'd make it up to you."

Wren exhaled then sighed. "It's not your fault; at least I know."

"Thanks; we'll take care of your hitch as soon as your bumper is repaired. We can make an appointment with the shop where we have all our repairs done unless you'd rather we took your truck somewhere else."

"That sounds good to me."

"Great; let's do your walk-through."

As the service manager opened the sliding door of the van on the passenger's side, Wren paused before she climbed inside. "Does it have an outside kitchen?"

The man's eyes widened. "This one does not; is that a deal-breaker?"

Wren smiled. "Not at all; an outside kitchen is great unless it's raining, cold, windy, or buggy."

The service manager nodded. "That was always my impression too, but some people want more room in the small trailers. The van has a propane stove, a microwave, a mini fridge, and a small kitchen sink. The bed is in the back, and it has a sleeping loft." He side-glanced at Wren. "I'm afraid to mention the bathroom."

Wren giggled as she climbed inside and inspected the camper. When she sat in the driver's seat, the manager gave her the keys. She started the van; after she adjusted her seat and the mirrors, she turned on the windshield wipers and lights.

"Since you're used to pulling trailers with your truck, the van will be simple for you to drive," the man said. "Do you want to take it for a spin?"

"I'll take a short drive around the parking lot, just to get a feel for it, then I'll unload my truck."

When she returned, the service manager asked, "What do you think?"

"It's really easy to drive."

While Wren unloaded her truck, Rascal remained in the van. After Wren put her backpack, computer bag, duffel bag, and a few kitchen items into the van, she stared at the box of stories.

"I don't have room for the box," she said.

"We could mail it home for you," the service manager said.

"That would work."

Wren and Rascal followed the service manager as he carried the box to the receptionist's desk.

"We need to mail this for Wren," he said.

The receptionist smiled as she handed Wren a notepad. "Write the address on this, and I'll put your box into a sturdier box for mailing."

Wren jotted down Betsy's name and the address for the Forgotten Oasis Campground.

"We'll get that out first thing in the morning for you," the receptionist said.

Wren sent Betsy a quick text then hurried back to join the service manager.

"All done?" the service manager asked.

"Yes, thank you."

When the service manager drove her pickup into a bay for its overnight stay, Wren climbed into the van's driver seat, and Rascal laid down between the driver's and the passenger's seats.

As Wren exited the RV dealership parking lot, she said, "We don't have far to go, which is nice; I'm exhausted."

After Wren registered and was settled at her site, she texted Justin. "At the campground in Mobile. Talk to you later."

"Let's check the restroom, Rascal."

When she went into the women's restroom, it had the distinct aroma of a pine-scented cleaning product. The dark tile floor felt gritty, but the two white sinks were gleaming. When she examined the two shower stalls, she frowned at the dirty grout in the corners.

While Wren waited for her Cajun food order to be delivered, she made her bed and put away her kitchen items.

She peered at the loft. "I could keep my clothes up there."

After she positioned the ladder and climbed up to the loft with an armload of clothes, her phone rang. She tossed her clothes on the foam mattress and scrambled down to grab her phone.

"You sound out of breath, honey. Are you okay?" Justin asked.

Wren rolled her eyes. "I'm at the campground; I was putting away my clothes."

"Why would putting away your clothes make you out of breath?"

"I'm fine; I was in a rush to answer the phone. The camper has a loft with a ladder that is supposed to be a second sleeping space; it's a perfect place to store my clothes."

"Tell me about your camper. Do you have a large RV?"

Wren giggled. "Not hardly; I have a camper van. It has a composting toilet but not an outside kitchen, so it's half a step up compared to the camper that was in the flood."

"What about writing? Do you have a place to write?"

"I have a small table with a folding chair and a faux leather recliner that's very similar to the passenger's seat with a tray that is big enough for my laptop, so I can actually write in comfort."

"That's great; when are you leaving in the morning?"

"Right after breakfast; it will take us a little over five hours with breaks."

"I'm supposed to warn you that Betsy will probably call you; Socorro implemented a new online reservation system at the Forgotten Oasis Campground, and it's giving Betsy fits. Sheridan said Socorro's not worried because after Betsy gets used to it, she'll claim it was her idea, but meanwhile, Sheridan said that Butch is lying low."

Wren snickered. "Butch knows his wife, doesn't he?"

"Sheridan said he's taking lessons from Butch because he hasn't yet learned to let Socorro work out her issues without trying to step in and help, or worse, crack a joke that she doesn't think is funny. I guess I'd better sit in on some of those classes."

"You only interfere a little bit," Wren said.

"That's what I told Sheridan, and he told me he used to think the same thing until he married Socorro."

Before Wren could respond, a car pulled up to her campsite; she said, "I ordered gumbo from one of the local restaurants, and my delivery is here. Can I call you back?"

"Call me when you're ready for bed, so I can tell you good night, honey."

After they hung up, Wren paid for her meal then fed Rascal before she ate.

As she took her last bite, her phone rang.

When she answered, Betsy said, "You have to come get me; I'll be your assistant and cook meals. Socorro has lost her ever-loving mind and installed an experimental reservation system that completely broke everything; while they were installing it yesterday, I spent the day working on getting you and Rascal back here. I have two schedules for you: one is camping in a tent, and the second one is staying at motels that allow dogs.

The only problem with the motels is that they all claim they will accept only small dogs, so I'll have to make some calls before we finalize on that one. I'll send you a copy, then we can talk tomorrow about what you want to do. Today was a nightmare: I spent the entire day calling people to make sure their reservations were correct."

"Were very many of them wrong?"

"Probably all of them were, but everyone was polite and told me their reservations were fine; why do people have to be nice?"

Wren swallowed hard to keep from laughing. "What does Butch say about the new system?"

"He's been busy with some enormous project, and I haven't seen him all day." Betsy snorted. "I don't think he even knows about it. My mother told me to never marry a man who is clueless, but I didn't listen, so I don't blame you; Justin has his moments too, doesn't he? You're eating supper, aren't you? I'll send you the email right now." Betsy hung up.

Wren shook her head as she gathered her trash from her supper. "I'm glad Justin warned me about Betsy, Rascal. Let's take a walk to check out the other sites and drop off our trash."

While Wren strolled to the dumpster with Rascal at her side, she said, "If we were in Hidden Gulch, I could help Betsy learn the new system, so she wouldn't be so upset."

As they toured the campground, Wren stopped at the site with a fifth wheel that was the same model as the one she and Justin had been discussing. Her eyes widened at how tall and long it was; she stared at the slide-outs and shook her head in disbelief. *There must be a lot of room in there.*

After they headed back to the van, Wren said, "The fifth wheel was much bigger than what I was thinking, but I might be comparing it to the tiny trailers and the van."

Wren set up her laptop and downloaded the schedule Betsy had sent her then checked the first two hotels that Betsy had on her list. "Hotels won't work for us, Rascal. We'd be happier camping, anyway. We'll get a tent and maybe a cot for me."

After she reviewed the camping list, she said, "Betsy's plan is for us to go from Mobile to Hidden Gulch in five days. It wouldn't be too much of a push to make it in four."

Wren stretched then wrote another chapter in her novel, "High Falutin' Killer", until she yawned and blinked to clear her blurry sight.

After she made her bed and changed into her pajamas, she called Justin.

When he answered, she said, "Rascal and I walked around the campground to check out the other campers; I saw a fifth wheel that I think was the size we've been talking about, and I was worried by how huge it was until I realized anything would dwarf what I've had for camping."

Justin chuckled. "I talked to the service manager at the RV dealership in Mobile; he expects to have your truck ready by Monday at the latest."

"While the campground reservation system was being installed, Betsy planned my itinerary for my return trip to Hidden Gulch. She found hotels that accept pets, but I know Rascal's larger than what they'll allow; we'd rather camp, anyway."

"Maybe I could take some time off and join..."

Wren interrupted, "Don't do that; we'd rather vacation in a fifth wheel later than camp in a tent while we travel to Hidden Gulch."

"What if we do both?"

"Do you have enough vacation for that?"

"That's my worry."

Wren narrowed her eyes. "Oh, really? Not up for discussion?" She feigned a loud yawn. "Guess it's bedtime for me."

"Sorry, honey, I didn't mean to keep you up so late; I'll talk to you tomorrow. Love you."

"Love you." Wren hung up then glared at the phone as she continued, "even though you make me mad."

Wren snorted. "I think I understand Betsy better; it really irritated me when Justin said his vacation was his worry like I was butting my nose into his business."

Wren rose from her bed. "I don't feel like sleeping after all. I'm going to write some more."

Wren opened her laptop and furrowed her brow. "Why do I have an email from Gage?"

Rascal rose and leaned against her as she read the email aloud. "Hey. Don't forget you have a blog due next week. You have comments on your blog to answer; I changed the settings, so you'll get a text at the end of the day with the number of new comments. Let me know if you want it changed back. Tara said I should have asked first."

Wren smiled. "At least Tara's still talking to Gage; that's the only good news I've had today."

When Wren opened her blog, she had seven new comments.

After she approved and replied to each one, she said, "I'll write a draft for my blog this week, so Kendra will have time to edit it. I've been wanting to add a new bad guy in my novel; I could write his back story in the style of flash fiction. He's a left-handed gunslinger, so I'll name him Lefty, or is that too cliché, Rascal?"

Rascal moaned in his sleep.

Wren nodded. "I'll take that as approval."

She pounded on the keys until she nodded off and her head jerked. Wren sighed as she stumbled to bed. *I'll work on it more tomorrow.*

Chapter Two

Wren opened her eyes when Rascal whined to go outside and jumped out of bed. "I didn't set my alarm and slept too late; it's already light outside."

As she rushed to dress, she grumbled, "I forgot to set up my coffee last night."

Wren and Rascal went outside for his break; while he ate his breakfast, Wren started her pot of coffee. "I was going to take a shower before I looked for somewhere to grab some breakfast, but now I don't have time."

After she drank half of her first cup of coffee, she made her bed and stowed her laptop before she poured the rest of the coffee into a travel mug and put her coffee maker into a cabinet.

While she entered the address for the Lost Pirate Campground into her gps, her phone buzzed a text from Justin.

"Good morning, sweetheart."

"What's good about it?" she grumbled as she responded, "Morning."

Her phone rang.

When she answered, Justin asked, "What's wrong?"

"Nothing." *What makes him so smart?*

When Justin didn't say anything, she continued, "I overslept."

"Have you had any breakfast?"

"I'll pick up something on the road."

"Eww," Justin said.

Wren giggled. "You've totally ruined my bad mood; I was ready to be cranky the entire day."

"I apologize." Justin chuckled then his tone changed. "But seriously, I have to apologize for cutting you off last night. I couldn't get to sleep because I was worried I was too abrupt."

Wren bit her lip then asked, "Did I get too nosy about your personal business when I asked about your vacation? I was interested, but maybe I need to learn to mind my own business."

Justin groaned. "I was afraid that was the impression I left; nothing is out of bounds for you to ask me. I was trying to tell you not to worry because I have plenty of vacation and a great team, but I guess I left out a few words."

Wren's smile was weak. "Just a few, but I should have asked what you meant instead of assuming the worst."

"Are we okay now, honey?"

"Almost; you owe me another I'm sorry kiss."

"You're right; I'll gladly pay up as soon as I can. Find some breakfast and let me know when you get to the campground. I love you, sweetheart."

"I love you too." Wren blinked back her tears as they hung up.

"Justin is so klutzy sometimes, but I jump to conclusions and get my feelings hurt when I take what he says wrong. This relationship stuff is hard, Rascal."

Wren sighed as she left the campground and headed east toward Florida; Rascal fell asleep on the floor close to Wren's seat.

After two hours, Wren stopped to refuel at a truck stop. When she pulled next to a pump, she smiled at a food truck at the edge of the parking lot next to the dog park.

"They've got shrimp po' boys, Rascal. You can investigate the dog park, then I'll pick up a po' boy and sweet tea for my breakfast and lunch and a homemade chocolate chip cookie or two for later down the road."

Wren ate half of her sandwich then wrapped the other half and put it in her mini fridge. "This van wouldn't be half bad if it had a real bathroom."

After Wren left the densely populated areas with high-rise condos and heavy traffic, she traveled through a desolate area of cypress stands, sand hills, and marshes with only an occasional dilapidated mobile home or ramshackle bait shop to break the monotony along the route.

When her gps showed the Lost Pirate Campground was ahead, she slowed then turned at a faded, wooden sign with a skull and crossbones.

She stopped next to a faded purple wooden building with a blue tarp over the roof and a large sea chest on the porch. When she and Rascal went inside, Wren glanced around at the well-stocked campground store; a deeply tanned woman smiled at Wren from behind the registration counter. Her long, dark brown hair was pulled back into a low ponytail and tied with a bright green bandana; her nametag said Taliyah.

"I'm Wren Weaver; I should have a reservation."

"You certainly do; it's for one week." The woman pointed at a map on the counter. "This is your site; it's close to the restrooms and showers. Mr. Hogue said you were a writer when he made your reservation; if you don't mind my asking, is this a writer's retreat for you? Will more writers be joining you?"

Wren smiled. "I'm a journalist, and I'm on assignment for a travel magazine."

"Really?" The woman's eyebrows raised. "That's hard to believe because we're not one of those destination campgrounds; there's nothing around here that would interest tourists. We have the natural Florida that people claim they want until they show up, but we don't have any of the amenities they expect. Our few guests are permanent residents who are retired or contractors and work in the area. So, what are you really writing about?" Taliyah peered at Wren. "Are you an undercover cop or a crime writer?"

Wren smiled. "Not at all; my assignment has been to write about lesser-known haunted campgrounds. The travel magazine has published three of my articles, and this is my fourth and last campground to visit."

The woman chortled. "Well, why didn't you say so? You've definitely come to the right place because you'd be hard-pressed to find a campground that's lesser known than we are. My dad founded the campground in the 1960s with a pirate theme because he was convinced he was a direct descendent of Captain Thadeus Hawthorne and wanted to honor the man who Dad claimed was the most successful pirate to roam the Gulf. Dad wrote the original Captain Thadeus Hawthorne story as a promotion for the Lost Pirate Campground, then an ad agency used it to write copy for five years of successful campaigns; I'll make you a copy and email it to you this evening if you'll give me your address." Taliyah pointed to a scrap of paper and a pen on the counter.

While Wren wrote, Taliyah continued, "When the first hurricane wiped out the campground, Dad worked hard to rebuild it, but the glory days were over, and after a second then a third hurricane, he gave up. I took over the campground because I loved it and wanted to honor his memory. I would have walked away the first day I showed up if it hadn't meant so much to Dad."

"Do you have plans to upgrade the campground?"

"Eventually; I can afford it, but unfortunately, I've been low on motivation. I'd like to read your three articles for inspiration; is that possible?"

"The travel magazine is online; you can read the excerpts, but the full articles are only available for the magazine subscribers."

"It might help me understand my potential customers and give me some ideas for where to start with my improvements if I subscribe." Taliyah pulled a business card from the holder on the counter. "Here's my business card in case you need to get in touch with me anytime, including after hours."

Wren smiled at the pirate logo on the campground card as she stuck it into the small pocket of her jeans before she and Rascal left.

After Wren parked her van at her site and plugged into the electrical outlet, she and Rascal roamed the campground.

They stopped at the women's restroom first; when she peeked inside, Wren said, "Looks okay and smells like it was recently cleaned."

They continued to the dog park that had doggie pick-up bags, a trashcan, and a water faucet with a water bowl hanging on a peg. Wren examined the yard to be sure there weren't any sandspurs.

"This isn't bad at all, is it, Rascal?"

After Wren opened the gate, Rascal trotted inside and investigated the grass along the chain link fence then ran off his excess energy as he raced around the perimeter. Wren relaxed on the wooden bench outside of the dog park until Rascal trotted to the gate.

As they continued their walk, they came to a lane at the farthest corner of the campground that was hidden from the rest of the campground behind some trees and found a section of old trailers with patio chairs, flowerpots, garden flags, and other items that had obviously been there for quite a while. The sites were wider than the sites in the main part of the campground, and many of them had old golf carts plugged into the electrical outlet to keep them charged.

A tall, muscular, middle-aged woman with gray streaks in her short, dark brown hair stepped out of a trailer but stayed in the shadows; she crossed her arms as she glared at Wren and Rascal when they strolled by.

Wren waved, and the woman nodded with no change in her facial expression.

After they returned to the van, Wren said, "The campground certainly has a lot of deferred maintenance, but at least the restroom was clean. I'm glad we came here; maybe we've helped Taliyah out of her slump."

While she ate the other half of her shrimp po' boy, Wren asked, "Did you find it curious that Taliyah asked if I was undercover or a crime writer? I wonder what crime there would be around here to write about. I'll have to ask her."

Rascal snuffled in his sleep.

Before she finished her lunch, her phone rang.

When she answered, Betsy asked, "Did I call at a bad time? Am I interrupting you? Do you want to call me back when you aren't so busy? I just had an urgent question, but it can wait. I'll talk to you later."

"Slow down, Betsy. Now is a perfect time. I just finished eating lunch."

Rascal raised his head and narrowed his eyes; Wren turned to gaze out the window to avoid Rascal's disapproving glare.

"How are you going to publish 'High Falutin' Killer' when you finish it? I know Kendra is your editor, so you have that covered, but do you know anything about publishing? Is that something you want me to do? I don't know where to start. Is it hard?"

"Do you remember Virginia? She and her husband own the apple orchard in Tennessee. She's researching self-publishing for me. We'll study the basics together and collaborate on a schedule, so I can move forward."

"Good, because I enjoy reading the stories."

"I'm glad you do because you see things that would never have occurred to me."

"Really? I have to go; there's something in my eye." Betsy hung up.

Wren finished her po' boy. "Let's walk to the beach."

As they neared the water, Wren wrinkled her nose at the fishy smell that reminded her of sulfur. "Some algae must have come in with the tide."

When they reached the beach, Wren stared at the intense, green water. "Now I see why it's called the Emerald Coast. I always thought the Gulf was blue; what makes it so green? I'll have to look that up later."

As they walked along the waterline, the tide was going out, and red and brown seaweed was strewn along the wet sand.

Wren pointed to the tiny holes in the sand. "Those might be ghost shrimp or small crabs."

Rascal stalked the sanderlings as the small birds darted across the beach in front of them.

"Leave them, Rascal," Wren said.

Rascal flopped down on the sand but twitched his tail as he continued to watch the birds. Wren scanned the horizon then peered along the shoreline ahead of them. "There might be a cove in front of us. Feel like going a little farther, Rascal?"

They hiked along the beach until they reached a small inlet. "It's too overgrown for us to explore any farther, but I wonder if there's a small marina around that bend."

As they walked back, Wren said, "Now, I'm not sure where the campground is. I know we walked past some sea oats, but there are sea oats all along the dunes. You're going to have to take the lead, Rascal, because everything looks the same to me."

Wren followed Rascal as he headed back; she waited on the beach when he was sidetracked and darted over a dune to investigate.

After they returned to the van, Wren refilled Rascal's water bowl and pulled out a bottle of water for herself. "I need to carry a red bandana so I can mark where we go onto the beach. The campground store had a wide variety of items, which was a surprise, but I didn't see any bandanas. I wonder how far away the nearest stores are; we'll have to ask the next time we go to the office."

While Wren sipped on the water, she re-read then edited her blog. When she was satisfied, she emailed the draft to Kendra then researched the Emerald Coast. "This is really interesting, Rascal; the green water is from microscopic plankton."

Wren read more about plankton, then found articles on the legend of sirens and shipwrecks.

After an hour, Wren stretched. "I certainly got lost down a rabbit hole, didn't I? Let's see if Taliyah is still at the office, Rascal; after that, we need to buy some groceries."

When they reached the office, Taliyah's car was gone, and the door was locked. Wren sighed. "I should have thought about it earlier; I'll see what I can find nearby."

Wren pulled out her phone from her pocket. "I found a store fifteen miles back the way we came; let's go."

As they continued to their campsite, Wren frowned. *There aren't any other campers in this part of the campground, and I didn't see any notes on the door for late arrivals.*

When they reached the grocery store, Rascal waited for Wren outside the door. She picked up two pieces of fried chicken, a ham and cheese sub, a small premade salad, and two packets of salad dressing from the deli then added bread, butter, and a small carton of six eggs to her cart. *That's about all my little refrigerator can handle, but it will last me for two days at least.*

After Wren and Rascal returned to the van, she said, "I'm a little nervous about staying in a rundown place without an owner or manager onsite, but I'll be fine because you'll let me know if there's a problem."

Wren put her items that needed to stay cold in the van's mini fridge before she headed toward the campground.

After she parked and plugged in, Wren fed Rascal then put some of the salad into a bowl, added a little salad dressing, and a piece of fried chicken on a plate. While she was eating, she glanced outside and shuddered as the sun slipped closer to the horizon. She immediately pulled down all the privacy shades then finished eating her chicken and salad before she set up her computer to write.

Wren peered at her email and raised her eyebrows. "I have an email from Taliyah."

She opened the email then downloaded the attachment.

"It's a photocopy of a handwritten document that is titled 'Captain Thadeus Xavier Hawthorne, A Fierce Pirate and a Master Sailor', by Eugene Hawthorne."

Wren rolled her eyes as she read; when she finished, she said, "The first paragraph is Mr. Hawthorne's glowing self-assessment of the article and self-congratulations on his writing talent. I don't know a lot about writing biographies, but I don't think that's a common practice. I'll read the rest of it to you; it's interesting."

Rascal put his chin on her knee and gazed at her as she read.

"In the 1600s and early 1700s, the pirate Jean Lafitte had a stronghold near New Orleans that was an established site to receive stolen goods. Lafitte's suppliers were privateers who were typically commissioned by the English or Spanish governments to attack enemy ships and pirates who were independent freelancers. Privateers and pirates alike stashed their bounty in marshes and inlets on the Florida coast where the heavy navy warships could not maneuver before they made a run to sell their goods to Jean Lafitte.

"Pirate Captain Thadeus Xavier Hawthorne was one of the most successful pirates of all time; no one crossed Captain X. He was tall, heavyweight, and fierce. His leathery face was scarred from combat, and he'd lost sight in one eye, but there was no eyepatch for him; pirates said he could see into your soul with his blind eye. He was highly regarded as one of the most skilled sailors on the seas because he read the wind, the clouds, the temperature, and the sea birds; Captain X could smell a Gulf storm and tell you how strong it was and when it would hit.

"The Spanish navy was certain they finally had Captain X in their cannon sights along the west coast of the Florida peninsula. Captain Hawthorne turned toward Mexico in an obvious attempt to escape, and the warship followed him. When he abruptly turned to the north then east to avoid a massive hurricane and made a mad dash for the coast of what we now know as the panhandle of Florida, he came so close to the Navy ship that the Spanish sailors trembled with fear in anticipation of the collision. The Spanish captain couldn't change course quickly enough to follow Captain X, and the lumbering warship was mowed down by the monster hurricane, with all souls on board lost at sea. The pirate ship was also assumed to have been lost in the storm, which meant Captain Hawthorne and his entire crew also perished; however, there were whispers among those who knew Captain X that he and his pirates outran the storm and made it to the Florida coast where they had stored supplies if they ever needed to lie low. The Hawthorne family of Sirens Beach, Florida, are direct descendants of Captain Thadeus X. Hawthorne as evidenced by…"

Wren was interrupted when her phone rang.

Wren glared at her phone. *Blake? What does he want? I thought I blocked that scum's number.* She ignored the call.

"Let's take a walk to the beach, Rascal; the odor of the decaying seaweed is an improvement over Blake."

Wren grabbed a flashlight as she left the van but had plenty of light from the bright, full moon as she headed toward the beach with Rascal at her side. When she neared the beach, she stopped. "Do you hear voices, Rascal?"

The low mumble of men's voices became clearer as Wren reached the beach. She listened for a few minutes before she followed Rascal when he headed back to their camper.

After they were inside the van, Wren called Justin.

Justin answered before the second ring. "Hi, sweetie; how's Florida?"

"Not at all what I expected; there's no one at the Lost Pirate Campground except Rascal and me and a few permanent guests, but they're so far away and hidden from sight, they are essentially at a different campground."

"No campers close to you at all? What about a resident manager?"

Wren bit her lip at the concern in his voice. "There isn't an onsite manager; I guess they can't afford one. My first impression when I arrived at the Bootleggers Campground in Tennessee was that no one was friendly; maybe I should give Florida a second chance."

"I don't like it."

Wren nodded. "I didn't expect you would, and I'm not so wild about it either, but I feel better telling you about it. The campground owner sent me a copy of the campground's story; I'll forward it to you."

Justin exhaled. "Will the story be enough for you to write your article?"

"It's great for background, but I still need a reason to encourage campers to come here; I'll see the owner in the morning because I have some questions about the area. She said she has some improvements in mind, so I'll talk to her more about that too. Tell me about your day."

"We hired a new deputy, and she'll start on Monday. She's a recent graduate, and her grandmother lives in Hidden Gulch. Her grandmother told us about her a while ago, so Pat used his contacts that he's developed over the years as a senior deputy to contact her two weeks after her training started and offered her a position with us. Her name is Jacqueline, but she goes by Jake. Pat and Jake plan to expand Pat's program for high school boys to include girls. Jake is bouncy, personable, smart, attractive, and all business when she needs to be. We were really lucky to get her before anyone else heard about her."

"She sounds great." Wren gritted her teeth. *Bouncy, smart, and attractive? I hate her.*

"She really is; Pat said all the high school boys and our county's young, single men are in awe of her."

"So, she's already well known in town?"

"She's been around off and on since she was a kid, but I didn't meet her until last weekend; several of us went out for coffee. I thought I told you about that."

Wren narrowed her eyes. *You didn't; all you told me about were the guys who wanted you to join the Arizona State police.*

Wren cleared her throat. "You probably did, and I've just forgotten. Were the Arizona state police interested in Jake too?"

"The state police? No, she doesn't have the experience to qualify, but I'll mention that to Pat because that's an excellent point. Not much of a chance of losing her, but we can't take any of our deputies for granted."

Wren furrowed her brow. "I'm confused; why are you so sure she'll stay with the county?"

"The pharmacist...wait, I did it again, didn't I? You don't know that Jake's engaged to our new pharmacist."

"That little tidbit does explain why she's so perfect for Hidden Gulch." *Maybe she's okay after all even if she is bouncy.*

"Thought so; when do you expect to wrap up your article?"

"I'll have a better idea tomorrow when I talk to the owner, Taliyah."

"Okay, and let me know if you need company at that deserted campground. I can be there in less than a day."

"I can't pull you away from work; Rascal and I are fine."

Justin chuckled. "Honey, we've had this conversation; when you say you're fine, I'm thinking I should hang up immediately and jump on the next plane to wherever you are."

Tears welled up in Wren's eyes, and her voice cracked. "I know, but not yet."

"Keep me posted."

They talked for a few more minutes then said good night.

Wren climbed her ladder and retrieved clean clothes for the next day.

As she stowed the ladder, she exhaled. "Rascal, I have an ugly jealousy streak that keeps popping up; I've never been like that before."

After she turned off the light and pulled up her covers to her chin, Wren listened to the distant voices while she worried about her character flaws and when Justin would grow tired of her. Her tears soaked her pillow as she cried herself to sleep.

Wren woke in the middle of the night when Rascal whined as a low rumble of thunder in the distance intensified. Wren shivered from the sudden drop in temperature and dangled her hand over the side of the bed to pat him, but he wasn't close.

She opened her eyes as a bright flash filled the van and coughed when a putrid odor swirled around her. Rascal stood near the small refrigerator while he stared at the van's side door where a translucent form glimmered.

A loud crack of thunder shook the van, and the apparition abruptly disappeared; the odor dissipated, and the eerie light dimmed then suddenly extinguished, leaving the van in complete darkness.

Rascal whined again; Wren pulled up her sheet to her chin for protection and rolled over.

"We were dreaming," she mumbled as she closed her eyes.

Chapter Three

When Wren sat up and raised the blinds next to her bed, the sky was dark blue. She rushed to turn on a light but whapped her left shin on her chair that she hadn't pushed close enough to the table before she went to bed.

Wren limped to the driver's seat where she had placed her clean clothes for the day and dressed in the dark before she turned on a light and started a pot of coffee.

She carefully examined the inside of the van then grabbed her staff. "Let's go to the beach and watch the sun rise, Rascal; I'm still a little shook from a bad dream."

While Rascal stalked sanderlings and investigated the sea grass, Wren gazed at the sky in the east as the dark blue lightened on the horizon and became streaked with pink and orange.

She flinched at the startling sound of her phone as it rang. *Justin.*

She immediately answered in a panicky voice. "Honey, are you okay?"

Justin exhaled. "I had a rough night and almost called you three hours ago because I had a strong hunch that I needed to talk to you, but I didn't know why. I waited until I thought you might be awake."

A tear slipped down Wren's cheek. "I had a severe case of melancholy and a restless night; Rascal has always been with me, so I've never felt lonely, but I realized how much I miss you."

"I knew I should have called." Justin exhaled. "We'll fix this because we belong together. I'll call you this evening but call or text any time; I love you, honey."

"Love you too. Sweet dreams."

After they hung up, Wren smiled as fresh tears streamed down her face. *Justin said we belong together, and he's right.*

Rascal cocked his head as he gazed at her.

"I'm okay; I need coffee. You need a special breakfast, and Justin needs sleep."

After Wren poured a cup of coffee, she fried an egg for Rascal and plopped it on top of his dog food.

"We're celebrating," Wren said as Rascal wolfed down his egg without touching the dog food before he ate the rest of his breakfast.

Wren hummed a joyful tune as she cleaned her pistol. After she was satisfied it was dry, clean, and protected from any damage from corrosion, she fried an egg for herself and toasted a slice of bread.

While she ate her breakfast, she checked her email. "Kendra has a few corrections and suggestions for my blog. After I put them in, I'll schedule my blog to publish next week, then we can go to the office to see if Taliyah is there."

After Wren updated and scheduled the blog, she and Rascal left for the office. On their way, a faded blue pickup truck pulling a long camping trailer stopped in front of the building. The driver mumbled to the passenger then headed toward the office. The passenger stood next to the truck with his arms crossed; he wore a wide-brimmed cowboy hat that Wren's dad would have called a ten-gallon hat, a western shirt with pearl snap buttons, and western boots with an ornate scroll on the sides and the patina of fine leather. Wren snorted. *He's definitely not from around here. He'd blend right in if he moseyed into Dry Creek, Texas.*

When Wren and Rascal passed by the truck, she glanced at the two fishing poles and the tackle box in the truck bed.

"I wonder if Captain X and his crew fished or hunted for their food around here, Rascal."

When Wren and Rascal went into the office, she examined the man's dark red scar that curved from the edge of his eyebrow to his jawline. *That scar is relatively new.*

Wren turned to the nearest shelf and examined the camping gear until the man left.

"Well, Ms. Wren, how did you sleep? It should have been quiet enough for you." Taliyah chuckled as she finished writing a note on a scrap of paper.

Wren smiled. "It was quiet; thank you for your dad's article. I have a million questions, though. When could I take up a little of your time?"

"Let's do it now. My two major chores are to clean the restrooms and dust the office, and I have all day to do them. Let's sit in my break room; it's a bit of a mess because I've been going through Dad's files. Would you care for coffee?"

Taliyah reached under her desk and pulled out a keyring loaded with keys. "I keep this on a hook under my desk. The keys are to the office, the breakroom, the golf cart, the storage room in the laundry, and my car. I have a tendency to forget where I put my car keys, so it's handy to have a spare around. I keep a set of car keys, my house key, and a key to the office door in my purse. Dad always kept his spare keys on the hook, so it seemed only right to continue the tradition."

Taliyah unlocked the door to the breakroom and invited Wren and Rascal inside. Wren gasped as she scanned the room. The walls were bright yellow and purple. A mural of a flamingo standing on one foot in the water at a beach and two dolphins leaping out of the water in the distance decorated the back wall. The mural on her left was oversized blue and green pots with pale apricot and neon pink bougainvillea blossoms; on her right was a scene of a 1950s style Florida cottage with a 1950s Chevrolet parked in front of it. The small yellow refrigerator that stood in the corner fit in with the overall theme of the room. Boxes were stacked on a small wrought iron café table and one of its chairs.

While Wren gawked at the room, Taliyah moved the boxes to the floor; she smiled as she poured two cups of coffee. "This was Dad's haven to recharge in between customers, particularly during tourist season. I'll never change it; it's like Dad is still around."

After Wren and Taliyah sat at the table with their coffee, Wren asked, "What was the draw for the tourists to come here?"

"Have you been to the beach? It's completely natural. Dad allowed only a few people on the beach at a time and had staff who made sure no one disturbed the sea oats or the dunes. Dad had a covered patio with a cabana bar and a small stage and an excellent sound system. He hosted local storytellers who told their stories about old Florida, and the guests loved them. Dad didn't want the headaches of running a restaurant, so he invited food trucks to sign up for exclusive nights."

"What about your plans?"

"I read your articles last night, and I was completely enchanted by your writing and inspired by your stories. I've been paralyzed because I was so certain no one would want to come here, and I couldn't face how disappointed my dad would have been if that were true. Doesn't make sense, does it?"

"It does to me; sometimes I fall into a trap of thinking the worst."

"That's exactly where I was until I read your articles. I have some old pictures of the campground; maybe they'll help you get a feel for Dad's vision of the campground. I pulled out the ones that I wanted ages ago; most of these are duplicates." Taliyah rose and pulled out a large envelope from one box and gave it to Wren.

"Thank you; I'll get them back to you later."

Taliyah joined Wren at the table. "I had a contractor lined up to renovate our sites, set up an area with utilities for food trucks, and rebuild our cabins and the covered patio with a bar, but I was overcome with the fear that it was a bad idea and didn't sign the contract. This morning, I forced myself to call him to see if he was still interested, and he is. I was surprised, but he told me he knew I'd change my mind; he's sending out a crew today to stake out the areas where they'll start working on Monday. I've been stumped by how to manage the beach because I didn't want it to be the Beach of Rules, which is what I called it when I was a kid. He had mentioned building an overlook deck so no one would actually set foot on the beach; we talked about adding that to the schedule."

Taliyah smiled. "I just needed a little push."

"I'm glad my articles helped you; thanks for telling me. I can understand why your dad was so intrigued by Captain X, but I'm not sure how the Lost Pirate Campground got the reputation of being haunted," Wren said.

"There's an inlet near here that is actually part of the campground property. Dad built a marina for small boats, and the campground became a destination for boaters to camp overnight or a day or two in one of our cabins. The first hurricane destroyed the marina. Dad tried to rebuild it, but it was never the same, and it's been years since it has been in use. The marina isn't accessible by land at all anymore because of all the overgrowth. I got offtrack; you asked me about haunted. People who stayed at the campground claimed they heard angry voices coming from the marina at night, even when no boats were there. The words were unintelligible, but everyone claimed the men were cursing; Dad said people liked to embellish their stories, but he still enjoyed repeating that Captain X and his pirates must have been haunting the area."

"Your dad sounds like he was a brilliant marketer; he definitely knew his customers, didn't he?"

Taliyah smiled. "Dad called me his secret weapon. It was my job to hang around the campground then tell Dad what people were saying; I learned to pay attention to the customer from him."

"What a wonderful legacy." Wren returned her smile. "The man that registered this morning had fishing rods in the back of his truck. Where is the best spot close by to go fishing?"

"I don't think we have any charter boats nearby that offer fishing in the Gulf. Locals sometime fish in the small creeks, but they mostly use cane poles. What kind of fishing rods did they have?"

"I'm not sure; I don't really know a lot about fishing, and I just got a quick glance. Do you think Captain X and his crew fished or hunted for food?"

"I would guess they fished, but there's a library in town next to the Baptist church; it's two blocks past the grocery store. I know at one time they had several local history books about the 1600s and 1700s because that was where Dad began his research on Captain X."

Wren rose to leave. "That's a great idea, and thanks for the coffee."

As Wren hurried to the van, Rascal trotted alongside her. "Maybe I'll have enough information to write a draft tomorrow."

After she disconnected the camper from the power source and put away the cord, she stowed her coffeemaker and cup in the cupboard and put her laptop in the computer bag.

On the way to Sirens Beach, Wren said, "I understand why the big RVs pull a toad; it's a hassle to unplug and secure everything when we leave, then when we return, I have to plug in the cord for electricity and pull out my laptop and set it up again."

When she stopped in a shady spot that was at the far end of the library parking lot, Wren said, "I'll leave the engine running so the van will stay cool. I won't be long."

Rascal circled his favorite spot in the middle of the van then flopped down and closed his eyes.

Before Wren reached the sidewalk, a man parked in front of the library; he had a mustache and a short, neatly trimmed beard and was only a few years older than she was. He strode toward the library with two books in his hand; when he reached for the door, he glanced back and smiled as he waited for her then opened the door for her.

Wren returned his smile. "Thank you."

When she went inside, Wren gazed at the well-worn wooden shelves with their neatly stacked books while she inhaled the distinct aroma of almond and vanilla that reminded her of an old book shop she had once visited in the Appalachian mountains. The red and green floral carpet was worn in spots and faded, but the library was well lit, and the recently painted, pale cream walls added to the welcoming ambiance for readers.

The man put his books on the desk then headed toward the back of the library.

A tall, pale woman stood at the desk with her back to the door while she talked on the phone; she had bright blue hair and tattoos on her arms. After she hung up, she turned toward Wren. Even though she was overweight, the skin at her neck and jowls drooped. "Are you Wren? I'm Laura. Taliyah Simpson called and said you're interested in the same books that her mother's ex-husband used for his research on the 1600s and 1700s; she assumed I would know exactly which books they were; I'll show you what I think she meant."

The librarian chuckled as she led the way to a section at the far corner of the library. "I've never met Ms. Simpson, but she's not the first to assume all librarians are over eighty years old. She said you're a journalist. Are you writing a historical article about Sirens Beach? Besides the very factual but dry history books and papers, we have a collection of gossipy letters from the mid-1700s; the former librarian told me before she retired that Mr. Hawthorne spent quite a bit of time studying them. They might give you a sense of the culture."

Laura pulled four books from the shelf and handed them to Wren. "The former librarian kept the manila envelope with the letters from the 1700s in a folder inside the file cabinet behind the desk. I've never bothered to look at them, and no one's asked about them since I've been here, so I'd completely forgotten about them until Ms. Simpson called. Is there anything else you need?"

Wren smiled as she glanced at the spines of the books. "This is great."

When they reached the desk, the man who had come in at the same time as Wren was waiting to check out a book. Laura scanned Wren's books then the man's book. She pulled out a folder from the file cabinet and handed it to Wren. "When you're finished with the books, give them to Ms. Simpson; she said she'd return them to the library. You don't need to return the folder; I should have gotten rid of it ages ago."

The man waited for Wren at the door and opened it.

After they were outside, he said, "When the librarian said you could leave the books with Taliyah, I wondered if you were the journalist Taliyah told us about who was writing a travel article about the campground."

"That's me; I'm Wren."

"I'm the architect on the construction project." He held out his hand. "I'm Dave Wyeth."

After they shook hands, Dave asked, "If you have time, could I buy you a cup of coffee? I understand you've visited several campgrounds; I'd like to get your thoughts on a couple of my ideas. There's a café in the middle of town only a couple of blocks from here; I've heard it's a great place to relax and have been meaning to go there. Ms. Taliyah said you travel with your dog; the café has a patio, so your dog could sit with us."

Wren nodded. "He'd like that; I'll follow you."

When Wren joined Rascal in the van, she said, "I'm going to have coffee with the architect for the campground construction project; he has some ideas that he'd like to discuss with a camper. Too bad he isn't an engineer with a RV manufacturer because I'd have plenty to say."

Wren followed Dave through a well-kept neighborhood of small, old homes on lots that weren't much bigger than the houses. "I wonder if there is a neighborhood association that takes care of the maintenance of the houses because their yards look so much alike; I'll bet these were beach cottages at one time."

Before they reached the café, Wren said, "Speaking of appearances, the librarian wore a gorgeous, well-made, blue wig and a short-sleeved shirt over one of those thin, long-sleeved T-shirts with tattoos on the sleeves that look so real that I thought at first her arms were fully tattooed. Laura is definitely shattering the librarian stereotype. She looks close to my age, but she's actually closer to fifty. If we were trying to solve a crime, she'd be my number one suspect because she's trying to disguise her age. I was a little confused at first when Laura referred to Taliyah as the daughter of Hawthorne's ex-wife, but Eugene Hawthorne would have been Taliyah's stepfather, so maybe the two of them were close even after the divorce; Laura might just be a stickler for details."

After she parked next to Dave's car, Wren inhaled the aroma of freshly baked cinnamon rolls as they neared the café.

"We'll have to have whatever they just pulled out of the oven and coffee," Dave said.

"I agree," Wren said.

After they were seated on the patio, the server brought their coffee and cinnamon rolls and a bowl of water and a treat for Rascal.

Dave pulled out a notepad from his backpack. "I'm interested in your thoughts about what makes a campground stand out. The general contractor is particularly interested in what might be thought of as extras that will have a big impact. We already have plans for all the sites to be level, wide enough so that no one feels cramped by their neighbors, and long enough for the big rigs plus their towed vehicles; we'll upgrade to two bath houses with laundry rooms and a large pool, but what could make the campground special?"

Dave took notes while Wren talked.

"Two dog parks, for starters: one for big dogs and the other for small dogs. A bonus would be a trail or a path where dogs who are used to being off leash could get away from the camp sites."

Dave stopped writing. "I didn't think about a trail; one already exists that would be exactly what you're describing with only a little extra work. It's an old boardwalk. I understand it was originally a path in the sand but was replaced with the raised, wooden walkway so that people in wheelchairs or parents pushing strollers could enjoy the trail. It goes from the campground to the marina with a large loop near the beach that returns to a spot near the office. Only the portion from the campground to the marina is safe to walk on; the loop needs some work but wouldn't take more than a week to have it ready for campers. The contractor told me he'd planned to rebuild the loop after he finishes the cabana, so that's in the plan."

"That's interesting. The boardwalk is clear enough to get to the marina now?"

"More coffee?" the server waved a coffee pot from the door.

Dave raised his eyebrows at Wren, and she nodded.

"Sounds good," he said.

After the cups were refilled, Dave said, "There's some brush that needs to be cleared, but the hand railings are easy to see from the back of the bath house if you're looking for them. You might enjoy it; it's actually a pleasant walk. Ms. Taliyah said it was too dangerous for anyone to be on, but I walked it earlier this week to see if there were any boards that will have to be replaced; there is a small section where the boards have warped and splintered, but the walkway and the railings from the campground to the marina are as sturdy as they can be."

"Rascal and I really enjoy campground trails. You walked it earlier this week? How long have you been on the project?"

"A little over a month, but this is my first onsite visit because I was finishing up another project when this one started. My wife will join me in a couple of weeks; it's been hard for her to get away because she's in logistics. I rented a house on the beach to surprise her; she hasn't been here in at least ten years. What else can you think of?"

"Maybe this is already in the plans, but the bath houses should be well lit."

Dave jotted down a note. "Got it. Anything else?"

"I can't think of anything; what ideas did you have?"

"I was thinking it would be worth highlighting the Lost Pirate Campground name and the local history of being pirate territory. For example, my plan includes a deck that overlooks the beach so the beach will remain undisturbed; I'd like the deck to be the bow of a pirate ship. What do you think?"

Wren's eyes twinkled. "I think that's brilliant; I don't think anyone would miss going onto the beach if they can see it from the bow of a pirate ship; if you add a spyglass, the visitors could scan the horizon for other ships. The markers for the site numbers could be buoys, and the restrooms could be marked lasses and lads."

"Exactly; I was a little worried it would become dated, but pirates are timeless, aren't they?"

"It certainly gives me a theme for my article. Do you expect your plan to be approved?"

Dave grinned. "The owner has approved it."

"Do you have a timeline I could share with my readers?" She pulled out a notepad and jotted down her new email address associated with her new website and blog. "I haven't been in one place long enough to have business cards made yet."

"I do, but I'll clear it with the general contractor and the owner first." Dave pulled out a business card. "Shoot me a text or email if you have any more ideas."

As they strolled back to their vehicles, Wren asked, "You said your wife hadn't been here in a long time; is she from here?"

Dave chuckled. "I have a tendency to assume everyone knows what I know. Crystal is Eugene Hawthorne's grandniece. After Eugene died, the family had a sudden split, but I don't know why; it was old history by the time Crystal and I met."

"It seems to happen in the best of families sometimes," Wren said.

Dave asked, "Are you going back to the campground?"

"We'll probably stop at the grocery store."

"If I don't see you later, thanks for everything; you've been a big help."

After Wren stopped at the grocery store to pick up a few more items, she and Rascal returned to the campground. Rascal wandered around the campsite while Wren hooked up the van to the electricity.

Wren pulled out a camping chair and sat next to her van while she scanned through the books. When she finished reviewing the last book two hours later, she stretched. "I'll type up some notes, but we can walk down to the beach for a break after I put the books in the van, Rascal."

As Wren strolled toward the beach, Rascal dashed ahead. When she reached the water's edge, Rascal barked. She couldn't see him as he continued to bark. *Something's wrong.*

Chapter Four

She raced toward him as his bark turned to a howl. When Wren rounded a bend, she saw Rascal standing in the water next to a body. Wren put her head down and raced at top speed to join Rascal.

The man was lying face down in the water, but the tide swept past him onto the sand and slightly lifted then moved his body further onto the beach. Wren flipped him over and cringed at his swollen, disfigured face with open wounds then noticed the red scar; he gurgled then gasped for breath. She grabbed him under his arms and strained to drag him onto the sand.

As she tugged, he moaned; his mumble was barely intelligible. "Shot...tell ya who..."

Wren positioned him on his side then pulled out her phone and called nine-one-one.

"I found a man lying face down in the water at the Lost Pirate Campground beach. He's breathing now, but he has been badly beaten."

While Wren waited for help, she struggled to pull the man out of the water but lost her grip and fell in the water. She struggled to prop up his head as the tide rose and washed onto the beach.

The man's breathing became more ragged. Wren said, "Take in a good breath then breathe out. You're doing great."

When Rascal howled, she exhaled in relief. "My dog hears a siren; we'll have help any minute now."

Wren listened to the changing tones as the siren grew louder; Rascal dashed toward the campground and barked when the siren abruptly stopped.

The frequency of Rascal's barking intensified, then Rascal joined Wren as a deputy sheriff raced after him. The deputy briefly paused to talk on his radio then rushed to Wren.

"This was as far as I could get him out of the water." She sniffed back tears.

The deputy grabbed the man and dragged him to the dry sand then lifted Wren to her feet. When she put her weight on her left foot, her left ankle failed her, and she cried out; the deputy caught her before she fell.

Tears spilled down her cheeks. "I must have re-injured my left ankle when I tried to pull him out of the water."

"Do you want to go to the hospital?" the deputy asked.

"No, I'll ice it and stay off it."

The ambulance crew hurried across the sand and put the man on a backboard to carry him to their unit.

"He was face down in the water when I found him; he told me he'd been shot," Wren said.

"Did you catch that?" the deputy called out. "You have a possible gunshot wound and a near-drowning victim."

"Got it," a woman shouted as the crew disappeared with the man.

"Are you staying at the campground?" the deputy asked as he helped Wren walk along the beach.

"Yes; my camper van is near the office."

"Did the man say anything to you?"

"He tried; he told me he'd been shot and tried to tell me who shot him, but he lost consciousness." Wren shuddered.

"Have you ever seen him before?"

"He registered at the campground this morning."

The deputy side-glanced Wren and shook his head. "You're Wren Weaver, aren't you? Would you be surprised if I told you the sheriff got a call from a marshal in Arizona?"

"Yes, I'm Wren, and no, I'm not a bit surprised."

As they neared her van, the deputy said, "I didn't talk to the marshal, so I don't owe him an apology, but from what he told the sheriff, I thought the marshal was exaggerating and being a bit overprotective."

"He doesn't exaggerate, but he definitely has a tendency to be overprotective."

The deputy chuckled. "Doesn't seem like it to me; it's kind of like paranoia. If it's true, it's not paranoia."

Wren rolled her eyes. *Why do men stick together?*

After the deputy left for the office, and Wren and Rascal were inside the van, she examined her pistol. "My gun isn't wet; that's a relief, but my skin is itchy from the saltwater. I'll shower then clean my pistol; the humid, salty air can't be good for it."

She grabbed her shower bag and her walking stick then hobbled to the shower while Rascal stayed close and followed her inside.

While Wren waited for the running water to go from cold to warm, she snickered as she glanced at Rascal who huddled near the door that went outside. "Are you afraid you might accidentally be included in taking a shower?"

When they returned to the camper, Wren draped her wet clothes on the rungs of the van's ladder then stared at her phone. *Should I clean my pistol first? Do I text or call?*

She called Justin; when he answered, she said, "Rascal and I had an adventure. We went for a walk on the beach and found a man who had been badly beaten; he was face down in a few inches of water. I pulled him out as far as I could then propped him up; he was still alive when the ambulance left."

Justin exhaled. "I'm really sorry you found him because that must have been awful for you, but it certainly sounds like it was lucky for him you did. Can you tell I'm trying to be calm?"

"I love that you understand; I panicked because I was terrified by Rascal's bark when he found the man because I instantly knew something was terribly wrong."

"How are you doing now?"

"I'm relieved my pistol didn't get wet; I took a shower to clean off the saltwater so I wouldn't itch later."

"Just because your pistol didn't go into the Gulf water doesn't mean it's okay; you need to clean it right away because saltwater and the salty air are corrosive. The combination of salt, sand, and water vapor will rust the metal and ruin your gun quicker than you realize."

Does he think I'm completely ignorant when it comes to the care of guns? Wren gritted her teeth then growled, "Is that right?"

"Most people in Arizona worry about the blowing sand, but the saltwater particles in the air around the Florida beaches are far worse."

Wren put her phone on the table and crossed her arms and fumed as Justin continued his lecture on the impact of saltwater on metal and why the corrosion was particularly harmful for guns and rifles.

His voice finally trailed off, then he tentatively asked, "Wren?"

She jerked up the phone from the table. "What?"

"I went overboard, didn't I?"

"Straight off the end of the plank and into the dank, dark, deep."

Justin coughed. "Dank, dark, deep?"

Wren snorted to stop a giggle. "You better not be laughing."

"Oh, no, ma'am; I'm still mortified that I forgot how proficient you are with firearms."

Wren narrowed her eyes. *I'm not sure how sincere that was.*

"Good," Wren said, "then you'll be happy to know I was smart enough to use my legs, not my back, when I was pulling the man out of the water."

"Okay, so what else?"

"I twisted my ankle again."

"Will you stay off it so you can heal?"

"Are you insinuating I would go traipsing around on an injured leg?" Wren giggled.

"I seem to specialize in saying the wrong thing; I wasn't very subtle, was I?"

"It was pretty good for you. For your information, I went to the library and grocery store earlier, so I have books and pamphlets for research. My plan is to start my article later today or tomorrow, so I can send it to Betsy and Kendra on Sunday for a final edit."

"I'll check on your truck today to let them know you might be ready to pick it up on Monday; I'll text you its status."

"Thanks. I hadn't even thought about my truck."

"I got your back, babe."

Wren smiled at the pride in his voice. "Yes, you do."

After they hung up, Wren reheated a cup of coffee in the microwave; while she wrote her notes for her article and flipped through the library books for details, Rascal napped.

Two hours later, Rascal stretched then stood at the door; Wren grabbed her stick and hobbled to open the door.

When they went outside, Wren's eyes widened as she counted six newly arrived trailers and RVs occupying sites.

As Rascal sniffed around the van, Wren said, "I have the brace from when I first twisted my ankle in Tennessee. I'll put it on; if nothing else, it will remind me to be careful."

After Wren wrapped her ankle and put on the brace, she joined Rascal, who was lying in the shade next to the van. "I'm feeling nosy, Rascal; let's walk to the office to see if Taliyah knows how the man on the beach is doing."

Wren was careful to put her weight on her staff instead of her foot, so their progress to the registration office was slow. When they reached the building, the door was locked. Several registration packets were in the late arrival basket that hung on the door.

"She must have had another meeting with the contractor; judging from how quickly the campground is filling up, it must be too disruptive for them to meet in the registration office. I'm restless; let's check out the boardwalk."

Wren stood behind the restroom and laundry building and peered into the brush. "I don't see any railings, Rascal. Dang it; tall men drive me bonkers sometimes. Can you find the board walk?"

Rascal trotted to the brush then turned and barked; Wren followed him into the high grass.

"Good job, Rascal." Wren scratched his ears then the two of them strolled slowly along the boardwalk as Rascal sniffed the air, and Wren held onto the railing and her walking staff as she peered at the sawgrass marsh and the floodplain forest of pines.

She heard the distinct whistle of a hawk overhead and shielded her eyes from the sun as she watched the bird soar on the thermals; it suddenly dived and disappeared into the trees then sharply veered upward with a long snake in its beak. The hawk's wings strained as they flapped to fly higher in the sky as the snake coiled. Wren's eyes widened when the hawk shook its head and flung the snake to the ground, then swooped down and flew away with the limp snake.

"This is really cool to have a front-row seat of the wildlife and ecosystem without worrying about quicksand or snakes unless a hawk drops one on you." Wren shuddered then scanned the sky. "Good; I don't see any more hawks. Is there quicksand in Florida? I'll have to research that."

Wren slowed her steps even more when she came to a section of warped boards on the walkway. "It's hard to walk on these planks."

She glanced at the trees when she heard a soft chuckle then shook her head. *It sounded like someone was laughing at a joke; must have been the wind.*

Wren continued gawking at the treetops and stumbled. After she hit her chin on the railing as she fell, Rascal nudged her while she sobbed on the uneven boardwalk.

"I bit my tongue," she wailed as she touched her chin then stared at the blood on her hand. "And cut my chin."

"Avast there, lassie. Ye be simperin' like a landlubber." A man's voice that was filled with the unlikely blend of authority and mischief rang out.

Wren sniffled as she sat up and tried to see who was speaking, but she retched as she inhaled an intensely sour odor.

When she regained her breath, she asked, "What's wrong with being a landlubber? Something stinks of old fish, and what is that disgustingly bitter smell?"

"Ye smacked yer chin, lassie, not your nose; why is your smeller out of whack? Fish is a fine meal that will keep a man from dying of starvation on the high seas, and rum and lime are the drink of life. Stop yer prissy bellyaching and haul yer sorry self up."

Wren groaned as she pulled herself up with her staff.

She blinked at the one-eyed man who stood in front of her with his hands on his hips. He wore a tricorn hat, a tattered shirt, leather britches, and buccaneer boots with wide cuffs; his cutlass dangled from his belt.

"Who are you?" she asked.

He threw back his head and roared with laughter. His spectral form shimmered slightly in the sunlight; he tapped his ghostly hat and replied with a voice that echoed across the marsh, "I be Captain X, the most fearsome marauder who has ever sailed the seven seas. And who might ye be, daring to converse with a spirit of the deep?"

Wren gagged at his foul breath. *Same smell as in my dream.* She held her breath then breathed through her mouth.

"I'm Wren, and I'm writing a story about the lost pirate, Captain Thadeus Hawthorne."

The captain instantly drew his sword from his side. "Lost? Did the scabby sea bass of a captain from the warship send you to find me?"

Before Wren answered, he peered at her; she met his gaze with a defiant glare.

Captain X returned his weapon to its scabbard. "Even though that cowardly bloke you hauled out of the water should have been tossed into the deep after he sliced the pirate's throat, you're not a traitor to the English."

"What pirate?" Wren asked.

"Go home, lassie; this is no place for a girl." Captain X disappeared.

"You aren't the first ghost to tell me to go home," she grumbled as she continued past the warped boards and on toward the marina. When they reached the marina, Wren stared at the refueling, washing, and repair facilities that contrasted with the deserted deck. "The marina is fully functional and in great shape, but there's no one here." Wren furrowed her brow as she studied the lamp posts that circled the deck. "Is this a marina that operates only at night?"

Rascal whined and returned to the boardwalk then stared at Wren until she followed him. Wren cautiously watched her steps as she returned to the campground; Rascal stayed near her side until they reached the end of the boardwalk, then he loped to the van.

After they went inside, Wren said, "It's way past lunchtime; I'm starving."

She made a sandwich and opened a bag of chips. While she munched, she searched the internet for more information about Sirens Beach and Lost Pirate Campground.

She raised her eyebrows as she read a string of articles from an old newsfeed. "Rascal, listen to this: Eugene Hawthorne, of Sirens Beach, was found dead on the beach near Lost Pirate campground six months ago; his murder remains unsolved."

Wren finished her sandwich and chips then nibbled on a cookie as she continued reading the newsfeeds. After an hour, she said, "This is what I've found so far: Eugene Hawthorne's throat was cut; the police didn't find the murder weapon or offer any explanation of motive. His ex-wife's daughter, Taliyah, took over the management of the campground after his death and continued to manage it while his estate was under probate. Eugene Hawthorne's brothers contested the will that he had signed right before he died, but all the assets went into a trust managed by his wife, Nadia, after the brothers quietly dropped their case. Taliyah's mother is reported to have recently retired in Aruba." Wren skimmed through the documents. "Nadia?

Where did she come from? Why did the brothers change their minds?"

Wren closed her laptop. "There's more to the Eugene Hawthorne drama, but I'll dig into that later. I'll shift to the gossipy letters."

After she read the first letter, Wren said, "This old letter is really hard to read. The words are pinched together, and I'm having difficulty following the thoughts because of the phrasing and spelling." Wren scanned four more of the letters then set them aside. "These are the same; I don't see any reason to look at the rest of them."

Wren read her unfinished draft for the Lost Pirate Campground and exhaled. "I'm not happy with this at all, Rascal; it would read better if it began with the campground and marina then pulled in the story from Eugene Hawthorne's article. I think I can tie it together with a wrap up of the intriguing mystery of Captain X and the voices from the marina."

She wrote an article about the careful preservation of the natural beauty of the beach and the plan to maintain it but still allow for campers to enjoy its beauty. She frowned. "It sounds too preachy; I think I'll send both versions to Betsy to see what she thinks."

Wren emailed the two documents to Betsy then called her.

Betsy answered on the second ring. "I just got an email from you, Wren; do I need to read that first?"

"No, I called to explain the email; I can't decide what direction to take with the article for the Lost Pirate Campground, so I sent you two versions."

"I'll read them then get back to you; do you have time to talk? It's a secret that Natalie and the new teacher are going to be engaged soon. I only know because I stopped to window shop at my favorite jewelry store in Tucson on my way to a sale at a new boutique. When I noticed Aaron and Justin were inside the jewelry store and standing in front of a display case, I waved; Justin must have said something because Aaron nodded then turned his back to the window; when Aaron's shoulders shook, I knew he was worried I had found out his secret, but there was no reason for him to fret because I wouldn't tell a soul. I waited until Justin came outside; he walked part of the way with me until we reached his truck, but Justin didn't say a word about what he and Aaron were doing in the store. When Justin opened his truck door, I asked him straight out if Aaron was getting a ring for Natalie, but Justin pretended he didn't hear me; isn't that the clearest proof in the world that I'm right? I have to make lunch to soften up Butch, so he'll spill what he knows."

Betsy hung up.

Wren rolled her eyes. "I didn't know the school board actually hired the male teacher from Phoenix, but they must have; Betsy said the new teacher's name is Aaron. I know Natalie is the server at the Watering Hole Diner only because Betsy told me earlier; Betsy saw Aaron in a jewelry store in Tucson, and she was convinced he was buying an engagement ring for Natalie."

Rascal opened one eye then closed it.

"It was exciting as far as Betsy was concerned, but it's hard to get excited about a secret when you don't really know the people, isn't it? Betsy said Justin was with Aaron; isn't it just like Justin to take the time to go to Tucson with the teacher who is new in town?"

Wren picked up the history book she had wanted to read more closely for details about the region during the 1700s.

"Let's sit outside; I can read a book in the bright sunshine, and both of us will enjoy the fresh air."

While Wren read, Taliyah joined her at the picnic table.

"I don't take enough time to sit and relax," Taliyah said. "Are the books from the library helping you?"

"They certainly are; Sirens Beach has a rich history of pirates, the rogues of the sea that appeal to everyone because of their reputation of being reckless, bold, and in their own way, heroic."

Taliyah laughed. "Makes me want to talk like a pirate."

Wren smiled. "That's exactly how I feel when I'm reading the history books."

Taliyah rose. "Thought I'd just stop by and check on you."

She took a step toward the office then paused while she cocked her head at Wren. "I can't remember if the library had any other material besides the books. Did the librarian mention anything else?"

"No, what else is there? Should I ask her for supplementary material?" Wren asked.

"Nothing that I know of; I was just wondering." Taliyah sauntered toward her office.

Rascal raised his eyebrows at Wren.

Wren rolled her eyes as she closed her book. "Don't be so judgy; I didn't want to get into a long discussion about the handwritten letters that are absolutely unreadable."

Wren rose, but before she went into the van, she glanced around the campground then squinted at the site where the man with the red scar had parked his long trailer. *The truck and trailer are gone; I wonder if the sheriff's office took it as evidence.*

Wren opened her laptop and searched for information about marinas. While she read, her phone rang; she answered the call from the library.

"Hi Wren; it's Laura from the library. One of our members in our readers' group reminded me you may not know about our Friday night fish fry suppers at the Baptist Church. I know it's short notice, but the group and I would like to invite you to be our guest this evening. It's casual; the church has inside and outside seating, but our readers' group eats at the library," Laura said. "Our group isn't very large; we have twelve members, but typically, only six to eight show up. Would you mind saying a few words to our group about yourself and writing freelance?"

"That sounds like fun."

"Excellent; if you'll meet me at five forty-five in the library parking lot, we'll pick up our food then return to the library to eat. Rascal is invited to join us; we love books and dogs more than people."

"That's great; we'll be at the parking lot by five forty-five."

"See you then. Before I go, have you by any chance seen Ms. Simpson today?" Laura asked.

"She stopped by my campsite earlier; why?"

"She called me while I was eating lunch and asked what resources I gave you; when I told her the history material I had from the 1600s and 1700s, she thanked me, but she sounded relieved. After we hung up, I kept thinking how bizarre it was for her to follow up on your research. What do you think?"

"Maybe she's worried I'll find some skeletons in her family closet, but I don't write the sensational, tell-all type of articles. She told me she had read my other travel articles, so she should have known my focus is on the campground."

"You might be right about the family reputation; I did an internet search when we heard a travel magazine was interested in the campground. After I found the legal documents that included a statement Mr. Hawthorne's ex-wife made and a collection of letters between Mr. Hawthorne and his ex-wife that were added to the public record during the probate court case, I saved the documents and letters on a library archive server. The letters discussed the campground and marina management and might provide more depth for the campground and marina in your article. I'll send you the link to the library's archive; you can decide if there's anything useful."

After they hung up, Wren said, "We're invited to a fish fry and to meet with a readers' group at the library tonight, Rascal."

Wren returned to her marina research; as she took notes, she frowned. "According to everything I'm reading, a marina could be very profitable. I wonder if it's called the Lost Pirate Marina? It should be. Dave said to text him if I thought of anything."

Wren sent a text to Dave. "Is the marina in operation? What is it called?"

He replied almost immediately. "Good questions; Sorry I didn't think of them first. Crystal will be here later this evening. Would you have lunch with us tomorrow? Noon at the café in town?"

Wren replied, "Sounds great."

"Our social calendar is filling up, Rascal. We're having lunch with Dave and his wife tomorrow."

Wren gathered her shower bag and a towel. "I was going to wait to shower until bedtime, but the fish fry and a meeting with a readers' group is a good reason to change my plan."

Rascal trotted alongside Wren as she hobbled to the restroom with her staff.

After her shower, Rascal's hackles raised as he stared at the office and gave a low, slow growl.

Wren's eyes widened at the faded blue pickup truck, and she shuddered.

"That looks like the truck the man with the scar drove." Wren hurried back to her van as quickly as she could.

Chapter Five

"I don't know why the blue truck bothered us so much," she said as she combed out the tangles in her hair.

After she dressed in her jeans and favorite olive-green shirt and secured her pistol in its holster, Wren checked her email and smiled. "Betsy has already read both versions."

She opened her email and read it. "Betsy likes the version that highlights the campground, but she said I should rewrite then include Captain X's story as the Lost Pirate."

Wren exhaled. "She's right; the full back story of Captain X is really Eugene Hawthorne's story and doesn't have much at all to do with the campground, so I'll get busy."

Wren began a story about pirates at the marina then sighed. "If the voices at night are ghostly pirates, are they unloading provisions or booty? We've got plenty of time to see if Taliyah's in the office; we can ask her."

When Wren accidentally put her full weight on her left foot, she winced at the pain; she stopped and held onto her staff with both hands before she continued with more care to the office. *This is annoying.*

When Wren neared the office, she saw the faded blue truck parked behind the building where it couldn't be seen from the driveway. She opened the door, but the office was empty; the break room door was cracked.

Wren cringed at Taliyah's shrill screech. "You have no business showing up here. You've been paid; now get out of here!"

Wren's eyes widened at the sound of a sharp slap.

A man growled, "You'll regret that."

Wren smelled the rotten fish odor as Captain X stood behind her and whispered, "Don't get caught here."

She stifled the urge to gag while she quickly and quietly closed the office door as Taliyah raged, "Don't threaten me."

Wren ignored her stabbing ankle pain as she hurried away from the office toward the paved path that led to the nearby restrooms. When she passed the blue pickup, she glimpsed the ten-gallon hat on the dash.

After she and Rascal were inside the women's restroom, Wren leaned against the wall as her heart pounded.

She inhaled then exhaled slowly to calm herself. "I didn't know I could move so fast. I'll splash some water on my face, then we can take our time while we return to the van."

As she headed back to her campsite, Wren glanced back at the office. *The blue pickup truck is gone.*

After they were inside the van, Wren gave Rascal a treat. "I don't know what the argument was about in Taliyah's office, but I'm perfectly happy with minding my own business."

She poured a glass of sweet tea and sat at her small table. "I'm still interested in the voices at the marina, but maybe someone in the readers' group knows the local legend."

When her phone rang, she smiled as she answered. "Hi, honey."

"I thought it would be more fun to call than text. Your pickup will be ready by the end of the day," Justin said.

"Really? That's great news; now, I need to finish my article."

"I thought you were finished or really close."

"It didn't feel right, so I wrote a second version and sent both drafts to Betsy. She liked the new draft but suggested incorporating pieces of the first draft into it."

"Sounds hard; what are you going to do?"

"It actually makes a better story; I'll have it ready for Kendra to edit before the end of the day tomorrow."

"Sounds like there won't be much of a change to your original schedule; you won't stay up all night to work on it, will you?"

"No, in fact, Rascal and I are going to the town's Friday fish fry then eat with the readers' group at the library. The librarian asked me to present a brief talk about my writing career after we eat."

"That's great, sweetheart; you always pick up a few more readers every time you talk to them face to face because you're so awesome."

"You might be prejudiced."

Justin chuckled. "Maybe, but I'm still right."

"I'm also having lunch with the architect for the campground renovation project and his wife, who is the grandniece of the original owner of the Lost Pirate Campground."

"I love how you found the right contacts so quickly; sounds like this article will be great."

"I hope so; what have you been doing?"

"Not much; just a little research and the usual meetings."

After they talked for a while longer, Justin said, "I need to let you go, so you can get ready for your Florida fish fry. Let me know how it is."

When they hung up, Wren sighed. "Can you believe we'll be heading toward Arizona next week, Rascal?"

Rascal yawned then circled his favorite spot and laid down.

At five, Wren put her laptop into the computer bag and secured all the rest of the loose items then disconnected the electricity. "We're getting low on dog food; if we leave now, we'll have time for a grocery store stop before we go to the library."

When she neared the gas station at the edge of town, Wren noticed the faded blue truck was parked at a pump. She quickly turned and stopped at the pump behind the blue pickup. Before she refueled, she pulled out the squeegee and washed her windshield while she glanced at the blue truck's license plate then frowned. *Florida license plate.*

She refilled her tank, but the man still had not come out of the store. She went inside the store and examined the snacks at the end of an aisle then finally purchased a small bag of trail mix. When she climbed into her pickup, the man in the Texas-style cowboy hat exited the store.

Wren pulled out her phone and examined it while she unobtrusively watched him as he returned to his truck. His face and arms were tanned and weathered from being outdoors; he wore sunglasses, but they didn't hide the crow's feet he'd developed from years of squinting. The man was middle-aged, medium height, and muscular. He scanned the area and the road then climbed into his truck and drove away without a glance at Wren.

She exhaled. "He looks like all the other fishermen I've seen lately."

When Wren reached the grocery store, a car pulled away from the lone parking spot with shade. After she parked, she said, "I won't be long."

Wren had three bags of groceries when she returned to the van and Rascal. "I have cookies, crackers, and cheese for me, and dog food and treats for you."

After she put the cheese in the refrigerator, Wren headed to the library.

Wren parked as close as she could to the front door, then Rascal followed her when she climbed out of the van. Laura waited on the front steps of the library and hurried to join Wren and Rascal.

"Are you doing okay?" she asked.

"I twisted my ankle last week then re-injured it today."

"Joints are so easy to re-injure, aren't they? Why don't I get our food to save you some steps?"

"I think a little exercise will help stretch the muscles if I don't put too much weight on my ankle."

"That's exactly what I think too." Laura matched Wren's halting pace as they strolled to the church.

When they reached the oversized tent where men were cleaning, breading, and frying fish in deep fryers, Wren raised her eyebrows when she saw the man with the expensive-looking Western boots as he deftly dropped fish into the hot oil, turned them, and removed golden, crisply fried fish from the fryer.

When he glanced up and noticed Wren, he smiled and nodded.

Wren swallowed hard then returned his smile.

"It's something to watch, isn't it?" Laura asked. "The menus are always the same, but nobody complains: fried fish, hush puppies, and coleslaw with your choice of red cocktail sauce or white tartar sauce. I suggest both. Our drink options are sweet tea or coffee."

"Sweet tea for me," Wren said. "Those men are so efficient; they've probably been cooking together for years."

"Most of them have; I think the man who is frying the fish must be a professional chef on a yacht. He shows up regularly and is always welcome because nobody fries fish like he does."

After they had their oversized, clamshell style, takeout containers that were heavy with food, Laura said, "The boy scouts will take our food to the library for us; we have several readers that order ahead because of mobility issues."

A boy in a cub scout uniform pulled a wagon while a gangly young man in a boy scout uniform walked alongside. The wagon held four of the large clamshell containers and a box with dividers for six large cups of sweet tea.

"Ms. Laura, can we deliver your fish dinners to the library for you?" the boy scout asked.

"That would be wonderful, thank you. We won't be too far behind you."

A golf cart pulled up next to them; the elderly driver smiled. "Can I offer you a ride to the library?"

While the driver drove the golf cart at a pace slower than it would have taken Wren to limp to the library, he kept up a running monologue about fishing and the thrill of dodging smugglers in the old days, but these days nobody knew how to fish, and the smugglers were thugs with no respect for fishing.

Rascal ran ahead and waited for them in front of the library.

Wren sighed. *I should have gone with Rascal.*

After they were inside the library, Wren heard voices from a room off the main lobby.

Laura said, "Our reading room doubles as our meeting room on Friday nights. We have four tables in the room, so I shift them around to form a square. We can seat twelve comfortably. If we ever had more people than that, we'd squeeze them in."

When they went into the reading room, Wren smiled at the five women and three men. Three of the women and two of the men were elderly; the rest of the readers were middle-aged.

After Wren was seated, she bit into the sweet, succulent fried fish.

"Isn't the fish good?" a woman at the table across from Wren asked.

"It's the best I've ever had." Wren took a bite of a hush puppy and raised her eyebrows. "This is delicious too."

Everyone smiled then resumed their conversations while they ate.

"One of our older readers wanted to tell you a story from her days when she was friends with Eugene Hawthorne, but she had a severe asthma attack and couldn't come after all. I promised her I'd tell you her story; it won't be as exciting as she tells it, but I've heard it enough times to share at least the important details," Laura said.

Wren nodded as she ate her last bite of fish.

After everyone had eaten, a woman and a man quickly cleared the table of cups, plastic utensils, napkins, and the now-empty plates. Laura raised her hand for silence.

"As you all know, our guest this evening is a talented journalist, Wren Weaver."

Laura smiled when she was interrupted by applause then continued, "Wren writes for a travel magazine and blogs. The library board approved a three-month subscription to the travel magazine and a two-year subscription as a sponsor of her blog."

While everyone murmured their approval, Wren raised her eyebrows. *I didn't know I had sponsors for my blog.*

"I've asked Wren to tell us how she became a journalist."

Wren smiled. "My real education began after I graduated from college. Writing was easy for me, but I had to learn to find topics for magazines that would interest their readers and to pitch my ideas to the publishers."

"That doesn't sound all that easy," one woman said.

"It wasn't at first; I spent a lot of time sitting at a café that had great Wi-Fi while I researched interesting jobs and learned the barista's elderly aunt had been an ice cream taster. The barista and I visited her aunt who told us incredible stories about ice cream. She said she would sneak homemade cookies into work and crumble them into her ice cream tastings to make the bites more interesting."

"Was she rewarded for creating cookies and cream ice cream?" a man asked.

Wren smiled. "No, she was fired; she was so distraught over losing her job that she went to the nearest bar, even though she didn't drink, and met a biker. They were married three months later and bought the bar where they met. Because of her discerning palate, they expanded their business to microbrewing and became well known for their craft beer."

"Is that a true story?" one woman asked.

"All of my stories are based on facts and legend," Wren said.

The readers laughed.

After Wren had answered questions for another twenty minutes, Laura said, "One last question, then we'll adjourn."

"What about fiction? Are you writing a novel?" a woman asked.

"That was two questions," another woman grumbled.

Wren smiled. "I never considered fiction because I was so busy writing articles for magazines until a friend challenged me to write a novel. It's quite different from writing short pieces, but I enjoy learning, and it's definitely a new avenue for me."

"When will it be published?" a man asked.

"I don't know; I haven't added it to my schedule," Wren said.

"Maybe it's time," another woman said.

"We all agree; on that note, meeting adjourned," Laura said.

A woman narrowed her eyes at Laura. "We'll be sending our author an honorarium, won't we?"

Laura smiled. "Of course; I'll include that in our minutes."

After everyone left, Laura said, "Wren, you were absolutely delightful. I promised you the story about Eugene Hawthorne. According to the most often repeated rumors, he was charged with smuggling ten years after he married Taliyah's mother. His lawyer negotiated a deal with the state, and the charges were quietly dropped; not long after that, Taliyah's mother divorced him. Our reader who was friends with Eugene said the rumors were wrong; he was protecting Taliyah because her mother was the smuggler, not him, which is why Taliyah is managing the property. The reader tells her story with more flourish that brings in intrigue and drama, but that's the bottom line."

"What was being smuggled? Drugs?" Wren asked as Laura accompanied her to the door.

"No one really said, but what else could it be?" Laura shrugged.

When Wren reached her van, she gazed at the deep orange sliver of light left on the horizon in front of the van. When she opened the back door for Rascal, Wren wrinkled her nose at the now familiar stench of rotten fish. She glanced up; Captain X stood on top of the van.

He had an old spy glass in his hand; he held it up to his eye and scanned the area. "It's a fine view up here, lassie; it's been a long time since I've been in a crow's nest. Grab the halyard and hoist the mainsail; let's push off for safer waters."

After Rascal hopped inside, Wren closed the door, then climbed into the driver's seat. "I think Captain X said let's get out of here; I'm having trouble keeping up with all the drama, Rascal. Maybe I can finish my article and we can head back to

Arizona without getting involved in anything; Justin would be happy about that, wouldn't he?"

As Wren cautiously headed toward the road, she rolled her eyes at the three solid thumps on the roof of the van.

"Hang on, Captain X." She sped to the road then maintained the speed limit until she cleared the town limit. She slammed her foot on the gas pedal and sped to the campground.

When she slowed to turn at the driveway, Captain X shouted, "Ye caught a good wind, there, lassie. You're a natural born pirate."

Rascal yipped then grinned when Wren glanced at him in the rearview mirror.

"Arr," she whispered. Rascal howled.

When she drove past the registration office, it was dark inside. The security light in front of the building created a circle of brilliance the surrounding shadows couldn't penetrate. After she parked the van, she held her breath when she opened the door, but when she climbed out, the captain was gone.

As she plugged the cord from the van into the electrical outlet, she exhaled. "I guess we're okay for now, Rascal."

Wren set up her laptop and added the story that Laura told to her Lost Pirate Campground side notes. After she fixed a cup of hot tea, she wrote her story about the ice cream taster then saved it in a new folder she named Sliver Stories. "What do you think, Rascal? I'm going to keep track of my off-the-cuff stories that have a smidgeon of truth to them."

Wren wrote the third version of her article that combined the first two, as Betsy had suggested. She read the new article and frowned. "Rascal, this needs a sliver story to give it a little punch. I have to clear my head; let's go for a walk."

Rascal led the way to the well-lit dog park where a collie pranced and investigated the perimeter. When they reached the dog park, Wren opened the gate, and Rascal sauntered to a corner away from the collie and sniffed the air. The collie tentatively strolled toward Rascal, but he ignored her and continued to sniff.

"Your dog is so calm," the woman joined Wren on the bench. "Jolie is a little nervous around other dogs because they either bark at her or are rambunctious."

"Rascal's the best." Wren smiled.

"When I first saw you and Rascal coming this way, I contemplated taking her back to the trailer. Did you see how interested she was in Rascal? I was a little surprised but decided to give her a chance to get acquainted, and I'm glad I did; she's enjoying Rascal's company. We're here for the weekend. One of my husband's old buddies lives not far from here; several of them are getting together to plan their fishing trip tomorrow, then we'll leave on Sunday. I'm looking forward to a little time to read and relax with Jolie."

"We'll be leaving Sunday too."

While they chatted, Wren glanced at a new arrival that drove past the registration office, and her eyes widened. *The blue truck and the trailer are back.*

She rose to stretch then sat on the bench at an angle that allowed her to observe the blue truck as it pulled into its same site.

The driver left his ten-gallon hat on the dash as he climbed out of the truck then disconnected the trailer from the hitch before he connected to the utilities. When he glanced around the campground, Wren casually shifted, so that her back was to him. She watched the two dogs until she heard his trailer door slam.

Jolie trotted to the bench; the young woman rose. "I guess Jolie's ready to curl up on the sofa while I read. My husband's buddy said we should stay close to the campground at night because smugglers use old marinas along the Gulf coast, and there is one near here."

"I always thought smugglers were a problem farther south."

The woman smiled. "I said the same thing; my husband agreed with me but told me his buddy said it might be a possibility because smugglers have fast boats and lots of fuel, and there would be very few patrol boats looking for them this far north. I'm still skeptical because fishermen are notorious for their tall tales."

After the young woman and Jolie left, Rascal nosed the gate. As they strolled back to the van, Wren said, "We took a little longer break than I expected, but I'm glad we did because talking about smugglers gave me an idea for a sliver story for the article."

After they were inside, Wren's fingers flew over the keyboard as she typed the story as a wrap-up to her article. "I'm sending this to Betsy to see what she thinks."

Wren emailed the revised article then brewed a cup of tea to celebrate. While her tea steeped, her phone rang.

"Hi, honey, how's everything?" Justin asked.

"I sent a revised article to Betsy; I think she'll love it."

"Nothing else?"

"You sound like a suspicious lawman, Marshal," Wren said. "For your information, I had supper with a readers' group at the library then told them a story before Rascal and I came home with Captain X riding on the roof of the van."

"Why did he do that?" Justin asked.

"I think he misses the thrill of the high seas."

Justin sighed. "Please don't tell me you sped back to the campground."

Wren smirked. "Okay."

Justin chuckled. "I asked for that one, didn't I? Did Captain X love it?"

"He said I was a natural born pirate."

Justin burst out laughing. "Your ghosts do know you well, don't they?"

"I wasn't quite sure if it was a compliment or an insult." Wren giggled. "What about you?"

"Typical Friday. While I sat in a typical boring meeting this afternoon, I was thinking about how much we don't know about each other; for example, how do you feel about surprises?"

"I guess it depends on whether they're good or bad; if you surprised me and showed up, that would be wonderful. What about you?"

"Same. The best surprise in the world for me would be if you and Rascal walked into the house, but everyone else had better call first if they expect a warm welcome. When I was nine, my dad's parents showed up at our house the day before Christmas Eve. I thought it was a great surprise, but Mom was confused because Grandma and Grandpa weren't spontaneous people. I heard Grandma tell Mom that my uncle, aunt, and four cousins who were younger than me had planned to arrive on Christmas day to surprise Dad. Grandma baked pies and Christmas cookies while Mom shopped for more food. Dad told me later that Grandma knew how Mom would have felt with no time to prepare for a crowd."

"Wow, your grandma had your mom's back. My family doesn't get together on holidays or any other time, for that matter. Mom talks about visiting relatives when she was a girl, but we never did, so I didn't grow up with a sense of family like she did."

"I don't think I've ever had a holiday meal with less than twenty people that I was related to," Justin said.

"Oh." Wren frowned. *That sounds terrifying.*

"It might sound overwhelming, but Dad taught me the fine art of eat then disappear when I was five," Justin added.

"When you were five years old?"

"It was easy because there were lots of kids, and Dad and I just walked out."

"Wasn't it a problem when someone missed you two?"

"Nope; Dad told me the trick was to blend in so well that nobody noticed when we left."

"I'm not sure that makes sense."

"Think about it; I think the idea will grow on you. It has really come in handy when I was investigating a case; I can teach you, and we'll blend in together."

Wren smiled. *Blend in together; that sounds nice.*

"That's okay, isn't it?" Justin asked.

"Of course it is, but you're going to have to do a lot of handholding, so I don't panic."

"Sounds like a plan, if you'll help me remember you don't mind the handholding."

Wren giggled. "We're a mess, aren't we?"

"Afraid so, but at least we can talk about it."

After they hung up, Wren sent a text to Gage. "Does my blog have sponsors?"

Gage replied, "Meant to tell you about that."

Her phone rang; she rolled her eyes as she answered.

Gage said, "I talked to Charlie; he included an ad for sponsors for your blog in the last travel magazine."

"Can we afford that?"

"Yes, it was no charge. Your articles have revived his magazine."

Wren frowned as she sat in her chair at the table. "Am I obligated to do anything?"

"Not at all; I suspect he's trying to get on your good side for a reason, but I have a written statement from him that the ad was strictly no strings, so you can do whatever you like. He did ask an odd question, though; he asked if I had any need of an editor."

"Oh, brother; what did you tell him?"

"I told him we had an outstanding editor; Mom overheard me, and she's making a Texas sheet cake for dessert."

"Yum; good move on your part. Did he say why he was asking?"

"He told me his nephew is an editor and looking for work. I told him we had a policy of not hiring relatives; Mom didn't hear that part. Charlie insinuated that you'd worked closely with his nephew, Drake, or maybe I got the name wrong; is that true?"

"His nephew is Blake; I thought he was my best friend in college, but he dumped me the second he found someone more glamorous who would be more useful in furthering his career. He's a lousy editor whose only skill is plagiarism. Can I afford you?" Wren asked.

Gage chuckled. "We should probably have a contract in place. I'll draw one up over the weekend and send it to you. Your dad's a lawyer, right? Have him review the contract for any revisions he'd suggest. We'll discuss money after your business grows to a point where you're ready to pay your staff, which I predict will be in less than a year; meanwhile, you're giving me the opportunity to use my marketing and negotiation skills while I learn the publishing business."

"The publishing side is all new to me too. Virginia Hudson from Tennessee has been sending me articles to read."

"Really? Do you mind forwarding them to me?"

"Not at all; I scanned the first few, but I'll have to start over and take my time to study the details."

"That's perfect; digging into the details is my forte."

"How's the campground coming?" Wren asked.

"Dad said he's ahead of schedule; I'm staying out of his way because he's the construction guru. I'll let you go, so you can send me those articles." Gage hung up.

Wren opened her laptop and forwarded all the articles she had received from Virginia to Gage.

She carried her laptop to her bed and propped up her feet to write in comfort. While she typed, she coughed, then gagged when she inhaled the now familiar stench.

Even though Captain X stood in the middle of the van at its highest point, he was bent over to keep from smashing his hat.

He sneered. "Aren't you the fancy lady with your feet up when you should be deciphering the enemy's plans the old pirate smuggled to you."

Wren squinted at him. "What plans?"

"The ones you have, lassie; have you become daft or has that strange box you wave your fingers over clouded your mind? Show her where the plans are, dog." Captain X disappeared.

Rascal rose, padded to Wren's backpack, and nosed it.

Wren threw off the blanket she had over her legs and huffed as she stretched to reach her backpack.

"I suppose the plans are in the folder, but I don't know what plans, and I definitely didn't understand anything else Captain X said."

She pulled out the folder and quickly read over each sheet of paper before she set it aside. After she'd reviewed the first five letters from the 1700s, she scanned four more. Her eyes widened at the next sheet of paper that looked like it had been printed on an inkjet printer.

"Rascal, Eugene wrote this letter to Dorthea." She continued reading. "He's accusing her of trying to cheat him by hiding funds that belong to the business; I assume he means the campground. He's threatening to divorce her and completely cut her out."

After she set the letter aside, she came to the next letter and snorted. "This letter is from Dorthea to Eugene; she's telling him he doesn't know anything about the business, but the style and wording match the letter from him to her. I think one person wrote both these letters."

Wren exhaled. "I guess this is what Captain X was telling me, except I still don't understand."

Wren read six more letters. "Each of Eugene's letters is more insistent than the one before; Dorthea's letters are advising him to back off if he knows what's good for him, which sounds like a threat to me. I might not have noticed the similarity in the letters between Eugene and Dorthea if I hadn't read the story written by Eugene Hawthorne, but the style is not even remotely close to his. I'm even more convinced that all the letters were written by one person, and it wasn't Eugene Hawthorne." Wren yawned as she read the next page. "This looks like construction notes. I'll read the letters again tomorrow when I'm not so tired."

Wren changed into her pajamas; after Rascal took his last break of the night, she crawled under the covers. While she drifted off, she heard three thumps on the roof of the van.

"G'night, Cap'n," she mumbled.

Chapter Six

Rascal whined; after Wren stepped gingerly out of bed and grabbed her staff, she and Rascal went outside.

Wren gazed at the trees and the dew-covered leaves that glistened in the early morning sunlight and smiled. "The trees look like they have jewels growing from the tips of their branches."

Her smile turned to dread as she stared at a formidable black bird that was perched at the top of a tree close to the van. It slowly flapped its massive wings then lazily glided toward the restrooms. After it landed on a branch that dipped from the bird's weight, more large birds appeared and gathered in the trees around the restrooms; the trees that had earlier been graced with sparkling gems were inhabited by the harbingers of death.

Wren shuddered. "Let's go inside, Rascal. It's creepy out here; I think those are black vultures that follow the turkey vultures who find carcasses with their keen sense of smell; they're probably waiting for enough of their own to show up to scare off the turkey vultures. We can explore later if we're feeling brave, or better yet, just ignore them and go into town for breakfast."

After they were inside, Rascal ate his breakfast while Wren texted Justin. "Good morning, honey!"

Wren answered her ringing phone immediately.

"What are you doing up so early?" she asked. "How did you sleep?"

"I slept really well. What about you?"

"Rascal and I slept straight through the night. What's on your agenda for today?"

"Jake and I are going on a hike early this morning, so I can assess her skills to see where she might need additional training before she goes on a back country rescue. Pat said I should tell you we always do that for any new hire. He and Jake will go to the range this afternoon while I cover the office and get a head start on next week's paperwork. What about you?"

"I'm going to catch up on my novel." Wren bit her lip. *And try to ignore some information that either is related to a cold case, or more likely, lies that are daring me to discover what they are covering up.*

"What else?" Justin asked.

"I'm having lunch with Dave and Crystal; he's the campground architect for their remodeling project, and his wife is the grandniece of the original owner of the campground. Gage arranged for an ad in the travel magazine for sponsors for my blog; he's going to send me a contract for Dad to review."

"How will that work with the sponsors?" Justin asked.

"You're asking the wrong person; do you want me to forward the contract to you too when I get it?"

"I'd say sure, except I wouldn't know what I was reading unless the contract mentioned cattle rustling or claim jumping."

Wren giggled. "I'll tell Dad to check for those two in particular."

"I'm glad your dad can review it for you."

After they hung up, Wren sat at her table with her laptop, a slice of toast, and a cup of coffee. "Let's see if Taliyah is in the office."

When they went outside, Wren said, "Taliyah's car is parked at the office. Maybe we can get an invitation to coffee, and I can ask her some questions."

When they walked into the office, Wren asked, "Do I smell coffee?"

Taliyah glanced up from her computer and jotted a note in a small notebook then tore out the sheet and slipped it under the keyboard. "You have perfect timing; I just put on a fresh pot. I stopped at the grocery store on my way here and picked up some cranberry-orange scones. Let's go into the breakroom."

While they sipped coffee, Wren nibbled on her scone. "I finished my article, but my publisher has a couple of questions for background, not for publication. I was hoping now would be a good time for you."

"Go ahead; what does he want to know?"

"Your mother's name is what? Dorthea? Where is she?"

"Yes, she lives in Aruba; we moved there when I was eight to be near her family after she and Dad were divorced." Taliyah helped herself to another scone.

Wren set down her cup. "Did you visit your dad very often?"

"I spent my summers with him until he remarried. One of Mom's friends from here told her that Dad's new wife was a lot younger than he was and wasn't very nice, so Mom asked Dad if it would be better for him to visit us, and he said yes. I never met the woman he married. Her name was Nadia, and Dad told me she was a shrewd businesswoman. He gave me some papers that he claimed proved how smart she was. I looked at them, but I didn't understand them when I read them the first time. After I came here to manage the campground for my uncles and saw the condition it was in, I didn't understand why Dad thought she had any business skills."

"I'm with you; did you see him after he re-married?" Wren asked.

"He came to see me one week every summer until the year before he died; he stayed with one of Mom's friends."

Wren smiled. "Sounds like you and your dad were really close."

"We were." Taliyah sighed as she refilled their coffee.

"Did you ever understand the papers he gave you?"

Taliyah snorted. "The marina was very profitable, but Nadia budgeted only minimal funds for campground maintenance. Dad said Nadia was an expert at research, and she told him that campers preferred a rustic campground. I don't think he saw how rundown it was."

Wren glanced around Taliyah's breakroom. "I didn't mention your dad's room in my article because I didn't know if you wanted to keep it private. I absolutely love it because it's a large room with a Florida flair. Have you thought about opening it up to your customers for a room where people could be social and meet other campers? You could call it Pirate's Cove, which is pretty lame; I'm sure you'd come up with something that's really catchy."

Taliyah tilted her head as she stared at Wren. "Dad would have liked that. What made you think of it?"

"I realized how much I enjoy sitting in here while we drink coffee and chat; it's a cheerful room."

As Taliyah narrowed her eyes and slowly scanned the room, she muttered, "Six round tables could easily fit in here without crowding, and there still would be room for a coffee bar and vending machines for cold drinks and snacks."

When Taliyah's phone rang, Wren rose from the table. "Thanks for the coffee, and the scone was delicious. We'll see you later."

After they returned to the van, Rascal circled his rug then flopped down while Wren opened her laptop and dived into the "High Falutin' Killer". Two hours later, she stretched then poured more coffee into her cup and sipped it.

"This coffee is too cold even for me."

While her coffee warmed in the microwave, she set her laptop on the floor and pulled out all the papers from the folder and separated out the documents and letters from the 1700s and put them on the floor with her laptop.

Wren sorted the letters from Eugene and Dorthea in her best guess of their intended order then read each one carefully while she took notes.

She was halfway through when Rascal whined. She glanced at the time on her phone.

"Yikes, it's almost eleven thirty; we need to get moving, don't we? We'll go outside for your break, then I'll brush my hair, and we can leave."

While Rascal explored the area around the van, Wren glanced around the campground before she turned toward the restrooms. Her eyes widened at the large branches that dipped downward from the weight of the birds. "There are even more vultures in the trees on the other side of the restrooms, Rascal."

On the way to Sirens Beach, Wren said, "I forgot to tell Justin about the vultures; I think I'm hoping they'll go away."

When they reached the café, Wren parked in front, then they went inside.

A server smiled and waved from a table she was clearing. "Rascal, your party is waiting for you on the patio. Just go through the French doors."

After Wren and Rascal went outside to the covered and screened patio and approached Dave's table, Dave grinned as he rose. "Wren, this is my wife, Crystal."

Crystal's long, black hair lay in ringlets around her shoulders and down her back. Her sunglasses perched on her head pushed the hair away from her face that was deeply tanned except around her eyes where the sunglasses had provided protection. She rose as Wren joined them, and the two women shook hands.

Raccoon eyes; Crystal spends a lot of time outside. Wren smiled. *Who was it that called the raccoon eyes troopers' eyes?*

"It's nice to meet you, Wren. When Dave asked for a table on the patio and added that we expected someone to join us, the hostess asked what the dog's name was."

Wren smiled. "That explains why the server told Rascal his party was waiting for him on the patio."

Crystal scratched Rascal's ears, and he flopped down between Wren and Crystal.

While they waited to order, Crystal said, "I read excerpts of your articles for the travel magazine. I never thought of the Lost Pirate Campground as being haunted; have you found anything for your article?"

"I always say my articles are based on fact and legend, so the answer is yes."

Dave and Crystal chuckled.

"I love it: fact and legend; tell me more about what you like to write," Crystal said.

"I've always written articles for magazines; I love diving into topics for the pleasure of learning more and sharing what I've learned. The collection of haunted campground articles for the travel magazine is the first time I've written a series of related articles, and I've really enjoyed it. I've branched out to blogging short stories, and I started writing a Western mystery. What do you like to read?"

"I love mysteries. How did you come up with a Western mystery?"

"I was inspired by a dear friend who left me a box of her partially completed short stories. Before she died, she asked me to use what I could. After I read the first short story, which was more of an outline with no defined ending, I felt driven to flesh it out and finish it."

"What a wonderful legacy."

Wren nodded. "Dave said you work in logistics."

"It's a dull job to talk about, but I absolutely love tracking products and making sure they arrive safely at the correct destination."

"What's your favorite product to track?" Wren asked.

Crystal peered at Wren. "No one has ever asked me that; you're definitely a very talented journalist. I'm not sure I have a favorite, but if I did, it would be one that was a challenge to track; think of products we see every day, like ice cream and coffee that the manufacturer quietly downsizes without notifying the consumer, retailers, or even other departments in their organization. They appear briefly in a large group but are quickly divided into small groups until they disappear individually into homes everywhere."

Dave stared at Crystal then cleared his throat as he shifted his gaze to his menu. "The pastrami sandwich sounds interesting to me."

Wren studied her menu then sneaked a peek at Dave and Crystal as they exchanged a look.

"I think I'll try the fried fish sub," she said.

Crystal pointed to her menu. "I'm with you, Wren. It says the fish is the catch of the day."

While they ate, Dave talked about the construction project.

When he took a break to eat, Crystal said, "I'm going back with Dave while he works this afternoon. I thought I might walk to the marina; do you have time to walk with me, Wren?"

"Rascal and I would enjoy it; I still can't move very fast, though, because I twisted my ankle yesterday. Unfortunately, it wasn't the first time this month I've injured that ankle, so I'll have to take it easy. I forgot to put on my brace this morning."

"Are you sure? I hope you don't feel you have to go; I didn't mean to sound bossy." Crystal furrowed her brow as she bit her lip.

"I would really enjoy it; you weren't bossy at all."

Their server stopped by their table; her hands were behind her back. "Ready for dessert? It's fresh key lime pie."

Wren and Crystal groaned.

Dave grinned. "Make that three to go."

The server set three to-go containers on the table. "You got it."

She gave their check to Crystal. "Here you go, ma'am."

Dave stared at Crystal. "That was sneaky, and so was our server."

The server laughed as she left the patio.

Crystal flipped her hair. "I know. Wren, we'll be at the campground later. I'll come by your van."

As Wren and Rascal headed back into the café to go out the door, she heard Dave ask, "Ice cream and coffee?"

"They just popped into my head."

After Wren parked at their campsite and connected to the water and electricity, she wrapped her ankle and put on the brace.

"The vultures are still in the trees, but there aren't quite so many of them. I don't know if that's good or bad, Rascal."

Rascal laid down on the floor where he could watch her.

While she waited for Crystal, Wren opened her email and cheered. "We heard from Betsy, Rascal."

She read the email. "She likes the new version but included a few revisions. After I put those in, she suggested I send it to

Kendra for a final edit. Betsy's becoming really cautious, isn't she?"

Wren quickly revised the third version then sent Kendra a text. "I have the final for the Lost Pirate Campground. Do you have time to edit it?"

Kendra replied immediately, "I would love to. Send away."

After Wren emailed the article to Kendra, she received the email from Gage with the contract. She wrote a quick email to her dad asking him to review the contract; after Wren forwarded Gage's email, she rose to answer the knock at the door.

"Perfect timing." She opened the door.

"My timing is always perfect. Are you going to invite me in?" Blake asked.

Wren slammed the door.

Chapter Seven

"That was a good one, Wrennie." Blake stood outside near the door as he chuckled. "I knew you'd be surprised, but I didn't expect you to surprise me back." Blake cleared his throat. "Seriously, I'm here because we have a great business opportunity."

Wren locked the door with a loud click; Rascal growled.

"Good idea to lock your door to keep your dog from getting out. You need to be careful; vicious dogs sometimes turn on their owner."

Rascal snarled.

Blake continued, "Are you okay in there with that dog? I heard about a group of investors that needed someone to write a series of articles about their new resort near Miami from the viewpoint of different age groups. I sent them copies of your first two campground articles, and they were sold on the idea. We'd stay at their resort; it will be my gift to you as payment for your work. I'll represent you, edit your articles, and submit them. I've already signed the contract."

"You are out of your mind, Blake; go away," Wren growled.

"I knew you'd be excited; I'll give you a chance to pack then be back later because we fly out of Tallahassee in the morning; you'll need to get your ticket before five o'clock. You've got people to leave your dog with, right?"

"If you return, I'll call the sheriff."

Blake chuckled. "You always had the best sense of humor. Pack your nice clothes if you have any; it's a posh resort."

Rascal snarled then barked until Blake left.

"Good boy." Wren hugged Rascal.

She sat at her table with her laptop and wrote a scene with a disreputable villain that closely resembled Blake. After forty-five minutes, she read over what she'd written. "I was going to kill him off, but I decided it's better to watch him suffer."

Rascal whined at the light tap on the door.

Wren smiled as she opened the door. "Hi, Crystal."

Rascal hopped out of the van and leaned against Crystal; she rubbed his ears and kissed his nose. "Wren, I'm really sorry I'm later than I expected. We ran into a completely obnoxious blowhard at the gas station. I'd tell you I had to pull away Dave before he punched the guy in the nose, but it was me; Dave said I had to talk to you first. Ready to go for a stroll?"

As they neared the restrooms, Wren pointed at the trees. "I see only one or two vultures; the trees were filled earlier."

When they stepped onto the boardwalk, Crystal said, "Dave told me some planks are warped, so we'll have to take it slow."

Rascal trotted ahead while Crystal walked slowly next to Wren, who clutched her stick with one hand and held onto the railing with the other.

Crystal said, "The guy at the gas station claimed to be your boyfriend, and he was glad that he could be here with you because you used him as a sounding board and told him everything. He told me he wrote all the articles for you because you were such a weak writer, but he thought with his guidance, you might improve. I was biting my tongue, but I almost lost it when he said he felt sorry for you because you never learned how to act in social situations, and you never had any friends. Dave took my arm and dragged me to our car; he said I shouldn't beat up the creep without your permission."

Wren snickered. "You met Blake; I knew him in college. My heart was broken when he dumped me until I realized how lucky I was. You do not have my permission to beat him up because I get first dibs."

Crystal smiled. "Dave told me I couldn't take away the pleasure you'd have when you cut him down to size."

Before Wren could reply, she coughed at the intense smell of rotting flesh and breathed in through her mouth and out through her nose to keep from heaving.

Captain X blocked their path on the boardwalk. "Ye saw the vultures; there's a dead predator ahead. It died of lead poisoning, lassie."

"Are you okay, Wren? I think I smell something ahead," Crystal said.

"Dead predator," Wren gasped. "Died of lead poisoning."

"Lead poisoning? Is there lead in the water?" Crystal wrinkled her nose. "I just caught a whiff of a foul odor that reminded me of a decomposing animal. Is that the dead predator? Like an alligator? You stay here; I'll go check."

"No, I'll check."

Crystal exhaled. "I'd love to pull rank on you, but I can't. Why don't we check together?"

Crystal tried to hurry ahead of Wren, but Wren passed her. When Wren saw the ten-gallon hat in the weeds next to the boardwalk, she dropped her stick on the boardwalk with a loud clatter and grabbed Crystal's arm. "Stop, Crystal. The dead predator is a man."

Crystal jerked away her arm to continue without Wren, but Wren lost her balance, fell, and landed on her face on the rough boards.

"Oh, no; I didn't mean to knock you down. I am so sorry." Crystal jumped to help Wren to her feet. "Your nose is bleeding, and your forehead and nose are scraped." Crystal pulled out tissues from her small backpack.

While Crystal tried to blot the blood from Wren's face, Wren glanced down at her shirt and moaned. "I'm bleeding all over my shirt."

Crystal handed her more tissues; Wren swiped her face with the tissues then bent forward while her nose continued to drip blood. After she pinched her nose, she mumbled, "Not graceful, but ankle okay."

"I couldn't quite understand what you just said." Crystal picked up Wren's stick and put her arm around Wren. "I'll help you back to the restroom, and we'll clean you up."

Wren shook her head; when she released her nose, she said, "Let's check the predator before we go back."

"If I leave for a quick look, you'll just follow me, won't you?" Crystal narrowed her eyes at Wren then shrugged. "Let's go."

While Wren held the tissue against her nostrils to keep from dripping more blood on her shirt, she used her other hand to hang onto her stick to keep from putting too much weight on her left foot. Crystal hovered; Rascal ran ahead.

Rascal barked then ran back to Wren and wiggled in between Wren and Crystal.

"Are we protecting you, or are you protecting us?" Wren asked.

Rascal growled, but stayed close to her.

When the odor became almost unbearable, Crystal pointed at the swampy grass on their left. "I think I see an alligator; it's not moving."

Captain X stood in front of Wren and pointed to her right. She turned and peered down into the muck next to the boardwalk then leaned over the railing for a better look. "There's a body under the bridge that has sunk into the mud and is half-buried."

Crystal joined Wren and stared. "Those are expensive boots."

Wren narrowed her eyes while she shifted to see where Crystal had pointed. *I know those boots.*

She pulled out her phone from her pocket and moaned, "I'm getting blood all over my phone."

After Wren told the dispatcher what they'd found and where they were, Crystal said, "Let's go back to the campground. You can rinse off the blood from your face and hands in the restroom; I'll show them where the body is."

"I'd appreciate that; do I look like I got into a fight?"

Crystal glanced at Wren as they made their way back. "Sure do."

Wren rolled her eyes.

"There's his hat." Wren pointed when they reached the spot where she had fallen.

"We'll leave it," Crystal said. "Do you know whose hat it is?"

"A guy that was at the campground."

When they reached the women's restroom, Wren hurried inside and moaned as she peered at the mirror. "I sure did a face plant; my nose, chin, and right cheek and eye got the worst of it."

She ran the water until it was warm then gently washed her face and hands; after she wiped down her phone, Wren went outside where Crystal was waiting.

"I'm going to change my shirt," Wren said.

"I'll go with you; it's too creepy to be alone."

Wren hobbled to the van with Rascal on one side and Crystal on the other.

After Wren changed and came out of the van, Crystal said, "I can't tell you how sorry I am that I made you fall. Do you have any ice? It will help keep down any swelling."

"It wasn't your fault at all; I'll get ice from the office."

"I'll do that after I show the sheriff where the body is."

A sheriff's deputy car roared down the driveway. The young deputy's tires skidded on the gravel when he turned at Wren's row; he slammed to a stop inches from the van's front bumper.

"Who attacked you, Wren?" he growled.

"I tripped and fell on the boardwalk; do I look that bad?" Wren glanced at Crystal; Crystal nodded.

"I'll show you where the body is, Deputy," Crystal said. "We won't be long, Wren. Will you be okay?"

Wren nodded as she sat at the picnic table; Rascal stood close to her.

After Crystal and the deputy left, Wren pulled out her phone to call Justin, but it rang before she had a chance.

She sighed. *He beat me to it.*

When she answered, she asked, "Did you hear from the deputy?"

"He said you called in another body, but he didn't have any details. Are you okay?"

"I'm fine; I lost my balance on the boardwalk and landed on my face. My nose has stopped bleeding, so that's good."

"What did the paramedic say?"

"Not much."

"Oh, so the ambulance isn't there yet. Where did you find the body? Can you give me a quick summary, so I don't have to guess what I should be asking?"

"Crystal and I saw some vultures in the trees and investigated to see what they had found. We were walking on the boardwalk to the marina, and I saw the man's ten-gallon hat; I dropped my stick, lost my balance, and fell. Captain X told me a predator had died of lead poisoning and showed me where the body was."

"Lead poisoning? Could you tell if the man had been shot?"

"No, he was lying in a swampy area under the walkway, so I couldn't tell much at all."

"Do you know who he was?"

"I recognized his ten-gallon hat and his fancy Western boots; all I know is that he fried the fish at the church supper last night and was the passenger in the truck driven by the other guy who was killed."

"Who else knows that?" Justin's voice was tense.

"Other than the killer, just me, so far."

Wren watched as a truck with a surveyor logo painted on the driver's door parked in front of the registration office. The driver turned off the engine then picked up his cell phone and placed a call.

Wren's eyebrows rose as she heard a cell phone ring in the faded blue truck.

"If he was frying fish at the church, he..."

Wren interrupted. "The deputy and Crystal will be here soon. I'll talk to you later; is that okay?"

"Sure; get somebody to look at your face."

After they hung up, Wren rose to get a better view of the driver in the parked truck; when the ringing stopped in the blue truck, the middle-aged man put down his phone.

Wren glanced at Rascal who narrowed his eyes.

She whispered, "Don't be like that; they might be here any time. The phone must have rolled over to voicemail."

When the man climbed out of his truck and headed to the office, Wren slowly limped toward the paved path between the office and the restroom. She listened while he rattled the doorknob then tapped on the office window.

As she turned toward the restroom, the man said, "Excuse me."

Wren turned as he strode to her; she shifted her staff to her left hand and casually placed her right hand on her pistol that was inside her waistband under her shirt.

"I'm sorry to bother you; a guy sold me his trailer, and I was supposed to pick it up from him here. He said if he wasn't around, to just let the campground manager know I was taking the trailer. Do you know where the manager is?"

"I'm sorry, but I don't know; she's usually here most of the time, so she may be back soon."

"I have the guy's phone number; he told me to call him if he wasn't here when I arrived, but he's not answering. He's probably working. I looked for a contact number for the manager posted on the office door, but I didn't see anything."

"She gave me her card; I'll call her for you." Wren pulled out the business card; while she called Taliyah, she asked, "What does he do?"

"He told me he's a cook at a marina restaurant; are there any nearby?"

Wren smiled. "A lot."

"I thought about trying to find him, but it doesn't sound like that's a good idea."

When the call rolled over to voicemail, Wren hung up and gave the card to the man. "She didn't answer; you could leave a message."

The man tapped the number into his phone then returned the card to Wren. "Thanks, I'll do that."

Wren and Rascal headed toward the restroom. After they were inside, Wren said, "I didn't want to look like I was snooping to see what he was doing, even though that's what I was doing; we'll just hang out here for a bit."

Wren sighed when she stared at the mirror. "The abrasions on my chin and nose are awful, and the swelling under my right eye seems worse to me. I can't cover my injuries with bandages because that would be even more noticeable."

After she dampened a paper towel with cold water, she held it on her right cheek and eye. "That feels good; I guess I should ice it."

When Wren and Rascal left the restroom, she glanced toward the office. "Taliyah's still not back, so I'll have to wait to get some ice."

When they headed toward the van, Wren whispered, "The man is hooking up to the trailer where the faded blue truck is; I guess Taliyah had information for him, after all. You don't suppose..."

Wren was interrupted by a dog yipping; Rascal barked in reply then raced toward the dog park. Wren smiled when she saw the woman and Jolie. The woman opened the gate for Rascal; he dashed inside where Jolie waited until he was close to her, then she led him on a race around the perimeter.

After Wren joined her on the bench inside the dog park, the woman said, "Jolie has been watching for Rascal. While you were gone, a young man who told me he was a close friend of yours was at your campsite and just left a few minutes ago. He knocked several times, so Jolie and I wandered on over to chat; I hope that was okay. It was a little awkward because Jolie growled at him; I've never heard her growl before."

Wren grinned. "Jolie's a good girl. He's not a friend at all: close or otherwise; I never realized how abrasive he was until after we parted ways."

The woman exhaled. "I thought he was a jerk myself, so I didn't chide Jolie at all. He said he might come back later, and

I told him we'd watch for him. I think we made him nervous because he left right away; I hope that's okay."

Wren giggled. "It's perfect; I had told him earlier that if he came back that I would call the sheriff."

"He was lucky it was just my vicious collie and me that chased him off, wasn't he?" The woman peered at Wren's face. "Have you iced your face? Your right eye is swelling."

"I don't have any ice; I was waiting for Taliyah to open the office."

The woman jumped up. "I'll be right back."

The woman returned with a small plastic bag filled with ice. "Here you go; come by our trailer anytime for more."

"Thank you so much; I'm Wren."

The woman giggled. "I'm April, so now that we're on a first name basis, can I ask what happened, or is that too personal?"

Wren smiled. "I wish I had a dramatic, glamorous, or even tragic story, but I tripped and fell; I tried to catch myself, but I had twisted my ankle earlier this week, so when I shifted all my weight onto that ankle, I was doomed."

"Doomed is pretty dramatic almost to the point of tragic; you have my full sympathy."

"Thank you; I've enjoyed the break, but I need to get back to my writing. My current chapter has a bad guy dangling over an alligator pit while the rope he clings to is slowly breaking one thread at a time; I suppose you can probably guess who he is in real life. I'm looking forward to writing the next scene."

"Doomed?" April asked.

"Most likely," Wren said.

Wren moaned as she rose. "I'm really sore; I think it's about time to go, Rascal."

Jolie trotted alongside Rascal; when he stopped at the gate, she stood next to him.

"I guess Jolie would like for Rascal to walk her home," Wren said.

When they reached the trailer, April narrowed her eyes as she inspected Wren's face; when Wren fidgeted from the attention, April said, "I don't mean to hover, but you need to wash your face; you still have some dirt in your abrasions. I have a gentle soap you can use and some antibiotic cream we can apply. Come inside, so we can do a little wound care."

April ran warm water into a bowl and handed Wren a soft face cloth. While Wren gently washed her face, April pointed to areas that needed extra attention.

April poured out the water from the bowl then refilled it. "Now you can rinse. Your no-good, former friend wore the knock-off western boots that the gas station sells for tourists; the boots are supposed to be a copy of a famous El Paso bootmaker, but if you know western footwear, there are some glaring differences. Maybe you could work that into your story."

"It definitely has possibilities," Wren said.

April handed her a paper towel. "Gently pat your face dry; some of the open wounds are bleeding a bit." April pointed as Wren patted.

"How's that?" Wren turned her head for April's inspection.

"Much better; when do you see Justin?"

"Later next week."

"Practice a pitiful face, just in case," April said.

Wren rolled her eyes. "I'll try it, but he might catch on."

April giggled. "He's a keeper, all right."

"I think so too."

"Here's the antibiotic."

After Wren applied the ointment on her abrasions, she said, "Thanks for everything. I rinsed my face in the restroom, but I didn't do anything else."

"Take the antibiotic with you and put it in your first aid kit; we all need a little help now and then, don't we? Come by later for more ice; I know Jolie would enjoy another play date."

After Wren and Rascal returned to the van, Wren called Crystal. "I was wondering about the man's boots. You said they were expensive; could they have been knock-offs?"

Crystal said, "Interesting question, Wren; they were custom-made. My dad's hobby was leatherwork, so I recognized the workmanship. Why do you ask?"

"My novel is a western mystery."

"Ah, that makes sense; you're planning to use boots as a clue, aren't you?"

"What do you think?" Wren asked.

"I think it's perfect. Did you hear from your publisher?"

"Not a word, but that's typical for him. He must think if he waits long enough, I'll write another article he can publish."

"I hate to tell you, but I'm with your publisher on this one. I'd love to read more of your articles. Have you thought about going independent?"

"I'm working on it; I have a new website with a blog. My marketing guru is setting up a subscription service on the website, but right now, I'm a little fuzzy on the details."

After Wren hung up, Rascal raised his head and stared at her.

Wren sniffed as she opened her laptop. "Just because I asked doesn't mean I was hoping it was Blake; I was covering all my bases."

Rascal sniffed then closed his eyes.

I don't believe me either.

Two hours later, Wren stretched. "Let's see if Taliyah's back."

When Wren went inside the office, Taliyah glared at her. "Did you give that man my phone number?"

Wren cocked her head at Taliyah. "If you're talking about the man who bought the trailer, I gave him the campground's business card."

"It had my personal number on it; it wasn't yours to give away." Taliyah's jaw was clenched as she spoke.

Wren pointedly raised her eyebrows as she glanced at the business cards that were still in their holder on the counter. "I'm sorry for the confusion; it didn't occur to me it was a private number."

Taliyah jerked open a drawer as she swept away the holder from the counter and dropped it and the cards into the drawer.

Taliyah stared at Wren then cleared her throat. "Apology accepted. I didn't mean to sound so sharp; I was surprised is all. Now, how can I help you?"

"Do you sell ice?"

"No, I have a refrigerator case, not a freezer; is there anything else?" Taliyah turned toward her computer.

Wren and Rascal left the office.

"That was really odd," Wren whispered. "Taliyah runs hot and cold, doesn't she?"

As they went into the trailer, Wren's phone buzzed a text from Kendra. "Nice job. I sent you my comments."

Wren hurried to open her laptop; after she included Kendra's corrections, she composed an email to Charlie and attached her final article, then exhaled. "I wish Justin was here so we could celebrate."

She sent Justin a text. "Sent the final Lost Pirate Campground article to Charlie."

Justin replied, "Good."

Wren sighed. "He's in another meeting; he'll call later."

Rascal stared at her then the door.

"Good idea; I can get some ice for my face, and you and Jolie can play at the dog park."

Rascal yipped.

Wren patted her pistol at her waist and picked up her stick.

Before they reached April's trailer, April and Jolie came outside. Rascal yipped then he and Jolie raced to the dog park.

April held up a washcloth and a small plastic sack filled with ice. "I have your ice for you."

Wren wrapped the sack with the cloth and held it to her face as they strolled to the dog park.

April said, "Jolie was out hard in her favorite napping spot. When she suddenly jumped up and insisted she had to go outside, I grabbed the bag of ice I had in the freezer for you; she must have Rascal radar. How was your afternoon?"

As they sat on the dog park bench, Wren said, "I heard from my editor and sent the final Lost Pirate Campground article to my publisher."

"That calls for a celebration, doesn't it? What are you doing for supper tonight? Let's have a cookout, unless it's too cold or too buggy, then we can have a cook-in."

"Are you sure? I'd love it. What can I bring? I'm great at picking out bakery cookies and buying ice cream," Wren said.

April giggled. "I'm ahead of you on that. I went into town to go to the gym. Have you seen it? It's really basic, but I was surprised a town this small had one. After my version of an intense workout, I stopped at the grocery store and picked up coconut, pecan, and dried cranberry cookies, rotisserie chicken, potato salad, and rolls to surprise my husband whenever he shows up sometime late tonight."

"That sounds good; I didn't know there was a gym in town. Where is it?"

"It's only a block away from the library, but it doesn't have a sign; it's tucked in between the hardware store and the fancy boutique."

"I know where the hardware store is, but I never noticed what was next to it."

"It's small and basic; the librarian must go there regularly; she was lifting weights. She can out-lift me, that's for sure. That must be how she lost all that weight. She told me she's lost over thirty pounds and still has twenty to go."

"Wow, that's a lot, even for as tall as she is."

"My hat's off to her; it takes a lot of perseverance and determination to lose weight," April said. "I could stand to lose a few pounds, but I love dessert, so that's not going to happen. What's your secret, Wren?"

"I'm cheap and not that great of a cook, but I'm not interested in fast food, so my meals are pretty basic; my favorite meal is leftovers."

"I knew you were my people; we adore leftovers. I have some super easy recipes I'll share with you, if you're interested," April said.

"That would be great."

Wren's phone rang. "It's Justin; do you mind keeping an eye on Rascal for a few minutes?"

"Not at all, but don't go too far away, so I can eavesdrop." April giggled.

Wren smiled as she strolled away a few yards from the dog park. "Hi, honey."

"I was really sorry I couldn't talk to you when I got your text; I was dealing with a dispute between two neighbors, but that's resolved, so tell me what's your next step."

"After Charlie sends me confirmation that my assignment is completed, I can walk away with a clear conscience. If I don't hear from him by tomorrow, I'll call him as a follow up."

"So, when are you planning to leave?" Justin asked.

"I'd like to leave tomorrow, but it will probably be Monday."

"I'll check on your truck in the morning to be sure it will be ready for you."

"Thanks; even if it isn't, I can still leave here on Monday and stay at the campground in Mobile."

"I wish I was there, so we could celebrate the end of your assignment."

"I do too; I was kind of feeling sorry for myself except Rascal and I made friends with a woman and her collie who are staying at the campground too. April invited us to have supper with her and Jolie this evening to celebrate."

"I'm glad you and Rascal won't be alone; did anything else interesting happen today? Not that you haven't had more than your share of excitement."

Chapter Eight

"The most irritating thing today was that Blake showed up at my van and knocked; I was rude and slammed the door when I opened it and saw him."

"Blake? What did he want?" Justin growled.

"He wanted me to write some articles, so he could take credit for them; I told him I'd call the sheriff if he showed up again."

"Did he return?"

"Not while I was at my campsite, but when he returned later, he caught April's attention; Jolie, who never growls, growled at him. Actually, from what April said, I think she growled at him too," Wren said.

"How's your nose?" Justin asked.

"Not bleeding; April gave me an ice pack for the swelling on my cheek and around my eye. A big disadvantage of the small trailers and the van is no ice. I planned to get some ice from the office, but the campground manager was gone most of the day, and I didn't feel like taking my scratched-up face into town."

"Send me a selfie."

Wren snorted. "When I get around to it."

Justin chuckled. "Fair enough. Call me before you go to bed, so I can tell you good night. I love you, sweetheart."

Wren sighed. "I love you too."

"I'll see you next week sometime," Justin said.

"Right; can't be soon enough for me."

After she hung up, Wren stared at her phone then slowly returned to the dog park.

"Do you want to talk? Who is Justin? Is he as dreamy as he sounds?" April asked.

Wren raised her eyebrows.

April smirked as she pushed back her hair. "I might have forgotten to mention I have excellent hearing."

Wren rolled her eyes. "He's the marshal in Hidden Gulch, Arizona. I met him when I went to Arizona to write my first article, and yes, he's as dreamy as he sounds, but sometimes he's annoying."

"That's good news; if you went on and on about how perfect he was, I'd be worried."

Wren giggled. "No chance of that."

Rascal and Jolie trotted to the gate; Rascal whined.

"He is obviously starving," Wren said.

"Shall we eat in about an hour?" April asked. "Or come whenever you feel like it because we can be flexible; it's just a matter of warming the chicken for a few minutes in the oven."

"That sounds great; I think a hot shower or maybe a quick nap to ease my aches from the fall."

While Wren gathered her shower things, her phone rang.

"Is now a bad time to call?" Betsy asked. "You can call me back when it's more convenient."

"Now is great; how's your Saturday?"

"It's good, but I think there's something going on that you and I need to know about. I heard in the grocery store yesterday that Justin hired somebody to clean his house. Can you believe that? How dirty can a house be with only one person living in it? I told Butch at breakfast I thought Justin must be having an early midlife crisis, but Butch had a terrible coughing fit and had to leave the table."

"Is he okay?"

"He's fine; he grabbed some cookies on his way out. I called Socorro and asked her if she knew why Justin was throwing his money around; she said he was a grown man, and I shouldn't worry you about it. Are you worried?"

Wren rolled her eyes. "No."

Betsy exhaled in relief. "Good, because Socorro would be really mad at me if you were worried. When are you going to have something for me to read?"

"I sent the final version Lost Pirate Campground to Charlie; I'm waiting to hear when he's going to print the article, so I'll have proof my assignment is over."

"What if he doesn't want to print the article after all? Except that's nonsense because it's a great article. Tell him I said that."

"Thank you, Betsy; I certainly will if he gets balky."

"Did you get your tent, so you and Rascal can camp on your way back here? Are you leaving in the morning?"

"I have to take the van back to the dealership in Mobile, Alabama, first. I'll buy our tent in Mobile."

"After I check the weather, I'll update your route and make reservations at campgrounds where you can stay next week."

"You don't have to do that," Wren said.

"I know, but I want to be sure you and Rascal will have somewhere safe to stay each night. Actually, it would be better if I wait to make your reservation for that night on the same day you're traveling, wouldn't it? I can't tell you how many times I've had to juggle campsites because a guest wanted to change their reservation after they traveled farther than they planned or stopped to rest and got behind schedule. I'll work on it and send it to you as soon as I can." Betsy hung up.

"Do you think Betsy will settle down after I'm in Arizona, Rascal?"

Rascal opened one eye and grinned.

"You're probably right; I'm going to take the shower I promised myself. Are you staying or going?"

Rascal waited until Wren gathered her shower gear before he stretched then stood at the door.

As Wren limped to the restroom, she glanced at the office. "The lights are on; I guess Taliyah is catching up on her work."

Rascal stayed outside while Wren went into the restroom. Wren's eyes widened when she saw the woman who was a permanent campground resident standing at the sink as she washed her hands.

Wren smiled. "How ya doin'?"

The woman kept her head down and growled in a husky voice, "You need to watch yourself, girl; better yet, you'd be smart to leave here as soon as you can."

The woman slammed the door as she went out.

Wren stared at the door then peeked out to be sure the woman was out of sight before she opened it. "Come inside with me, Rascal. I can't take a shower unless you're in here to guard me. That woman's voice was creepy. It was like she was trying to sound gravelly to scare me. I thought everyone in Florida had a tan, but she was pale."

After Wren's shower, Rascal raced to the van and waited for her as she walked back with careful steps. When she opened the door, Rascal leaped inside. "I have a couple of questions for Taliyah, but I'll wait until tomorrow; maybe I'll catch her in a better mood than she was today."

Wren hung her towel on a hook in the van's tiny bathroom before she and Rascal headed toward April's trailer. She stopped and turned when a car engine started up behind her; Wren frowned as Taliyah's car sped toward the driveway. "I really don't understand Taliyah." Wren waved as April opened her trailer door, and Rascal raced ahead.

After she was inside the fifth wheel, Wren smiled as she gazed around the trailer. "This is a palace, especially compared to my rolling shoebox."

April snickered. "I'll have to remember that when I feel closed in with a stinky dog and an equally stinky husband after he comes in from fishing."

After April put the chicken in the oven to warm, she asked, "You don't have any plans to drive anywhere tonight do you? I have water, iced tea, and beer; I'm leaning toward a beer, since it's an indoor picnic."

"Beer sounds good."

After April gave Rascal and Jolie treats, she opened two beers, then set a bowl of dip, napkins, and two plastic knives on the table. While she slipped a sleeve of multi-grain crackers onto a plate, April said, "I love a good smoked fish dip, and the grocery store makes it fresh every day."

Wren smeared some dip onto a cracker and took a bite. "Mmm; this tastes great. How did you and your husband meet?" She added more dip to her cracker.

"Corky and I met in a law office parking lot. My granny wanted to sue her neighbor for tearing up her yard and running over her prize rose bush when the neighbor swerved to avoid hitting a turtle on the road. Granny said if the neighbor hadn't been speeding or had their phone in front of their face, they could have simply stopped and let the turtle continue on its way. Most neighbors would have worked it out, but Granny and that particular neighbor had been at war for years." April smiled. "You're welcome to use any part of Granny's story in a book if you need a long-running grudge match."

Wren chuckled. "Thanks; I probably will." Wren smeared a cracker with dip and took a large bite.

"While Granny was with her lawyer, who was a sympathetic listener who charged by the hour..." April paused and raised her eyebrows at Wren who covered her full mouth with her hand while she snickered.

April continued, "I sat in my car with the windows up while I read; it was not hot at all, and there was a bit of a cool wind from the north. I heard a woman screaming on the other side of the parking lot, so I rushed to see what was wrong. She had removed one of her sneakers and was pounding it on the driver's side window of a car. A man who pulled into the parking lot ran toward her too. It was really hard to understand her, but we finally realized there was a dog inside the locked car; she screamed it was dying from the heat. The dog was huddled in the back seat as far away from the driver's side as he could be. While the man tried to calm down the woman by explaining her shoe would not break the glass, and she was scaring the poor dog, I went to the other side where the dog was huddled. My original thought was to comfort the sweet pup, but on impulse, I pulled on the door handle and discovered the car was unlocked; when I opened the door, the dog jumped into my arms. The man laughed and told me I was amazing; the woman stomped away in disgust. That wonderful man was Corky; we found the dog's owner and went to a nearby coffee shop to talk trash about the whole incident."

Wren laughed. "I love it. I think that woman deserves a spot in my novel too."

"She certainly was a piece of work; tell me more about you and Justin." April put the potato salad and plates on the table before she popped the rolls into the oven to warm along with the chicken.

"It's not nearly as interesting as your story," Wren said. "Rascal and I were at a hardware store when a huge man came into the store and made some threatening remarks to the campground owner, so Rascal growled; the angry man left right away. Later, I was in a coffee shop, and the angry man came inside. He accused me of having a vicious dog and took a very aggressive stance as he resumed his previous threats. A sweet, elderly man rose from his table to come to my aid; I was actually afraid I was going to have to fight the angry man myself to protect the elderly man."

April chuckled. "I can just imagine."

"The marshal came into the shop; he didn't realize it, but his presence scared away the angry man. After the marshal picked up his order, he came to my table and asked if he could join me; I didn't know if I was going to be arrested or if he was being nice to a newcomer." Wren wrinkled her nose. "It's not nearly as dramatic as yours." *Except he asked me if I'd seen the ghost, Thomas, and was impressed that Thomas talked to me.*

"That is such a sweet story." April removed the chicken and rolls from the oven.

While they ate, April said, "Your angry man reminded me of what Corky told me earlier. He said the head of a major smuggling operation in the area was murdered years ago, and everyone assumed the business died with him until two known smugglers were found dead, so Corky's buddy said it's a power war. Corky asked his buddy if he was in the smuggling business because he's so up on all the gossip. All the guys, and even his buddy, laughed."

When April side-glanced at her, Wren giggled. "Corky's buddy is in law enforcement, isn't he?"

April's eyes widened. "How did you know?"

"Only two types of people understand criminals: criminals and law enforcement types."

April grinned. "And super smart journalists. Ready for dessert?"

Wren moaned. "I don't have any room at all."

"We're leaving first thing in the morning. When are you leaving?"

"Rascal and I will be leaving bright and early Monday." Wren glanced at the clock. "Oh dear, it's almost nine o'clock; Rascal and I should head out."

April handed Wren a large plastic bag that was filled with cookies and an equally large bag of treats for Rascal. "You'll need lots of cookies and treats on your travels; we'll keep in touch, I'm sure."

Wren hugged April. "Thank you so much; Rascal and I enjoyed your company."

Rascal yipped; Jolie grinned then yipped.

After the four of them went outside, April and Jolie stayed near their steps to watch Wren and Rascal as they returned to their van. When Wren opened her door, she turned and waved; April and Jolie went inside the fifth wheel.

"It's nice to have people who have our back, isn't it?" Wren glanced at the office. "The lights are on, and Taliyah's car is still there. I don't know if she'll be in tomorrow. Let's see what kind of mood she's in."

As Wren slowly hobbled to the office, Rascal stayed close. When Wren opened the door, Taliyah pushed her hair out of her face with the back of her hand.

"What brings you out so late, Wren?" Taliyah asked. "Oh, my goodness! What happened to your face? Did you run into something?"

"Kind of; my ankle gave out on me, and I fell flat on my face."

"Do you need some ice for your eye? Did you know it's turning black?"

"I iced it earlier; the swelling has gone down, but I didn't think about bruises. We just dropped by to check in with you; I'm planning to leave early Monday morning and wasn't sure if you'd be here tomorrow. I didn't want to leave without seeing you."

"You're so sweet. I've just finished getting all my records in place. It was nice of you to come by because I'm actually leaving first thing in the morning; I may have to stay up all night packing."

Wren stared at Taliyah's forced smile.

Taliyah continued, "I suddenly realized managing a campground is more stress than I can handle. I called my father's brothers, who are the owners of the campground, and they understand."

"What about all your plans?" Wren asked.

"They're more the owners' plans than mine, so all the renovations will continue. When I told them about your idea for the meeting room, they loved it. I just finished closing the books and sent a copy to the accountant. I planned to celebrate with a glass of wine. Would you like to join me?"

"I'd love to."

Taliyah locked the front door, then the three of them went into the breakroom. Taliyah pulled out two small paper cups and a full bottle of re-corked wine from a cupboard; after she poured wine into each cup, she handed a cup to Wren then raised hers. "Cheers."

"Cheers." Wren tapped her paper cup against Taliyah's then sat down at the table.

Wren coughed and her eyes watered when the now-familiar odor of rotten fish filled the room.

Captain X stood across the table from her; he pointed at her cup with his cutlass as he roared, "Don't let that blood of death touch your lips, lassie."

Taliyah took a sip and sighed before she drained her cup. She reached into the cabinet and pulled out a Lost Pirate tumbler; after she filled the tumbler with wine, she then set the bottle on the table as she joined Wren.

"What are your plans?" Wren set down her paper cup untouched on the table.

"I'm going home to Aruba to be with my mother. She has an accounting practice; she can finally retire if I take over the business. I love numbers; I'm not so much a people person." Taliyah drained her tumbler.

"I'm surprised you're leaving because I think you're very personable."

Taliyah smiled as she refilled her empty tumbler then paused as she peered at the bottle before she set it down. "More, Wren?"

Wren glanced at her small paper cup. "Not quite yet; it's very good, isn't it?"

Taliyah nodded. "It's my favorite; funny, I don't remember opening it. You're the first person who has ever stayed at the campground in a camping van. Isn't that a big hassle to unplug the electrical cord and put it away when you want to go into town for a quick grocery trip?"

"It's definitely a tremendous disadvantage; it does keep me from running into town as much."

"You're certainly welcome to borrow my car if you need to go to town for groceries or other necessities."

"That's really kind of you; thank you, Taliyah."

"It's nothing." Taliyah hiccupped. "Oops; guess I drank the last few drops a little too fast."

Wren picked up her cup as she furrowed her brow. "I wonder why Nadia didn't stay after your dad died. Where did she go?"

"Mom said Nadia didn't like to work, so she just walked away; Mom told me Dad's brothers wanted me to manage the campground, anyway." Taliyah poured the remaining small amount of wine into her tumbler.

"What about the marina?" Wren asked.

"Nadia was supposedly managing it, but Mom said it hasn't been in operation or properly maintained for years." Taliyah gazed into her cup. "I never thought I'd be leaving Dad's campground."

Taliyah burped. "'Scuse me. Nadia never really liked the campground. Dad kept the notes she wrote him about everything he did wrong in an envelope. One of her notes said he should sell the campground, buy himself a condo in Tallahassee, and buy her a beach house to live in while she managed the marina. Besides the notes, Dad kept a photo of him and Nadia at the marina; I guess he wanted to remember the good times when they were first married."

"I can see why he would want to remember when they were happy," Wren said.

Taliyah continued, "I've kept the envelope in a drawer near the register because Dad kept them, and I wanted to honor him. After I read the notes once, I never looked at them again because she was so mean. One of her notes told him he had to stop visiting me and Mom because the travel cost too much money." Tears rolled down Taliyah's cheeks, and she sobbed.

Wren shook her head. "Doesn't sound like she was very nice at all."

"She wasn't; Mom said Nadia's soul shriveled away because of all her nastiness."

Wren covered her mouth as she faked a yawn. "Excuse me. It's getting late, isn't it?"

"It is, and I should get busy. Thanks for stopping by." Taliyah's words were slurred.

Wren carried her cup with her as she and Rascal headed to the door. After she unlocked it, Wren called out, "Did you want to come lock the door behind me?"

"It'll be fine; I shouldn't have come here," Taliyah mumbled.

"What?"

Taliyah groaned. "Just leave."

On their way back, Wren said, "Taliyah is even more confusing when she drinks, but I think she will miss the campground more than she realizes, Rascal."

When Wren reached her van, she said, "I don't want to dump this on the ground because the bright red would stain the gravel and be too obvious. I'll take it to the restroom and pour it into a sink later." She set the cup on the ground behind the van's front tire. "It'll be okay there."

After they were inside, Wren put on her pajamas. She carried her laptop to her bed and fluffed her pillows for support before she propped up her feet.

Before she checked her email, her phone buzzed a text from April. "Here's a link to an article that talks about smuggling on the Emerald Coast of Florida. Thought you'd find it interesting."

Wren followed the link and read the article. "April was right, Rascal. The article says the international smugglers reacted to the pressure of intense law enforcement around Miami by moving their activities further up the coast and systematically eliminated the long-standing local smugglers who refused to cooperate with them through coercion or even murder."

Wren tilted her head. "I wonder if that's what happened to Eugene Hawthorne? Maybe that's why Nadia left."

She opened her email. "Well, we heard from Charlie; he said the article is fine, and he hopes we can work together again real soon. Fat chance, right, Rascal?"

She snorted. "He congratulated me on my new assignment, but he was surprised I was going to be working for Blake." She shook her head. "Did you catch the 'working for Blake'? I'm not responding to this tonight."

Wren picked up her phone and sent a text to Justin. "Are you working late?"

A few minutes later, he responded, "Will call later."

Wren stared at her phone. "He must be really busy. I'll write until he calls."

When her phone rang at midnight, Wren jerked awake, then fumbled to find her phone that had slid off her bed.

She cleared her throat before she answered, so she wouldn't sound as groggy as she felt.

After she answered, Justin said, "I'm sorry I'm calling so late; Jake has a test on Monday, and I was helping her study. Time got away from us."

"What kind of test?" Wren mumbled as she blinked her eyes and struggled to sit up.

"An English test; she's enrolled online for a bachelor's degree; she asked me if I'd help her."

Sounds suspicious to me. I don't trust Jake. Wren sniffed. "Betsy would have been a better tutor."

"I should have thought of Betsy."

"You're right. Where were you studying?"

"She came here, but because it was so late by the time we did all we could, I followed her home to be sure she would be okay."

"Is that so? Do you tutor any of your other deputies at your house then follow them home?"

"Nobody else has ever asked me for help," Justin said.

"Really?" Wren's voice was icy.

Justin cleared his throat. "I think I'm getting your point. It looks like I'm giving her preferential treatment, and that isn't very professional of me, is it?"

"Nope, and she should have asked someone else or asked you for a recommendation."

"Pat said I've been acting like a pole cat, and I need to take some of the management classes the state offers. I'll sign up for the next class."

Pole cat? Wren bit her lip to keep from giggling.

"When?"

"First thing when I go into the office." Justin cleared his throat. "What about you? Did you and Rascal enjoy your celebration?"

Wren snorted. Not the smoothest change of subject, but I'll roll with it. "We enjoyed the celebration; April gave me a bag of cookies and treats for Rascal for our trip home. I saw Taliyah tonight. She's leaving the campground in the morning."

"That sounds like an impulsive decision."

"I thought so too; she's a bundle of contradictions. She talked about her father's brothers; I would have expected her to say her uncles. Taliyah's mother divorced Eugene Hawthorne after they'd been married for ten years; Taliyah said she was eight years old when she moved to Aruba with her mother, so wouldn't that imply Eugene was her father? Except the librarian refers to her as Eugene's ex-wife's daughter. I realize none of this is interesting to anyone besides me, but I can't help feeling that it has something to do with the two men being murdered."

"Is that going to keep you awake?" Justin asked.

"No." Wren pretended to stifle her fake, loud yawn.

"Good; how's your ankle?"

"Not bad; I'm taking it easy."

Rascal sniffed; Wren frowned at him.

"I love you; call me in the morning when you wake up, so we'll be even," Justin said.

Wren giggled. "Fair enough; love you too."

After Wren hung up, she heard the voices from the marina.

"Hear that, Rascal? I'm wide awake now; let's see if we can spot any ghosts besides grumpy Captain X."

Wren dressed and patted her waistband where her pistol rode. She grabbed her stick and dropped her flashlight into her backpack before she stuck her phone in her back pocket. After she put on a brown plaid long-sleeved shirt, she and Rascal went outside.

An occasional wispy cloud drifted by and briefly blocked the bright moonlight while the cicadas, katydids, and tree frogs sung a chorus of impending rain. The salty night air was damp; Wren's hair stuck to the back of her neck in ringlets. When a mosquito buzzed her ear, Wren whispered, "I'll be right back."

Wren went inside and sprayed herself with the natural mosquito deterrent, then she and Rascal headed toward the boardwalk.

The voices became clearer as Wren and Rascal neared the marina. Wren crouched down when she saw the small boat tied to the marina. *If they were pirates, I'd call it belayed.* Wren covered her mouth when she snickered at her own joke.

She watched as two men unloaded the cargo onto a trailer hitched to the golf cart.

"I thought I saw something." The man, who was short and overweight, paused and stared in the direction where Wren and Rascal crouched before he handed the large carton from the boat to the tall, emaciated man who waited on the marina platform.

"You're always seeing things, Fat Tony; don't slow us down by getting all spooked."

"I don't get spooked, Sticks," Fat Tony whined. "I'm more cautious than you are; who saw that snake the last time we unloaded? It wasn't you."

Sticks snorted, "That wasn't hard; you always see snakes that I never see because they aren't there."

"This box got crushed." Fat Tony frowned at the box as he lifted it off the boat.

Sticks walked the box into the now-abandoned bait shop. "We'll get it later; I don't want to deal with any complaints tonight."

"What about a shortage?"

"Shortages aren't unusual; boxes fall overboard all the time."

Fat Tony asked, "Aren't we going to haul two loads?"

"No, that's too much trouble; if you'll walk alongside to keep the boxes steady on the trailer, we can do this in one load."

"Why do I have to walk? My feet hurt, and I don't like it here; this is the creepiest place we've been."

Sticks growled, "You can do it in two loads if you want, but it would take all night. I'm not making two trips if we can do it in one, and you're getting on my nerves. Let's just get this over with."

Wren smelled old fish, stale rum, and lime as Captain X knelt next to her and whispered, "Tomorrow's the day, but for now, lassie, git ready to hightail it to your landlubber dinghy. The wind's in your favor, lassie; they won't hear ye and dog."

Sticks took the driver's seat and Fat Tony walked next to the trailer as they headed away from the marina to a path through the woods that Wren hadn't noticed before.

"Go," Captain X hissed.

Wren picked up her stick and raced back to the van with Rascal running behind her to cover her back.

When she was inside, Wren realized she had cried in silence the entire way from the pain in her ankle as she ran. "I knew I was going to be sorry when I ran as fast as I could, but Captain X wanted us out of there fast, Rascal."

While Wren sat on her bed with her arms around her knees, she rocked and moaned from the pain. Rascal jumped onto her bed and licked away the tears from her face. She wrapped her arms around him, buried her face in his neck, and sobbed at the intense pain in her ankle.

Her phone rang.

She answered and sniffled. "It's late."

"What's wrong? Something's wrong."

"Can I just say I miss you?" Wren pulled up her shirt tail and wiped her eyes.

"Yes, but there's something else."

"Sometimes I don't follow instructions, and sometimes I do."

"Are you okay now?"

Wren sighed and smiled. "Yes."

"If you don't feel safe, leave."

The tears flowed down Wren's face; she sobbed. "I love you." She slowed her breathing. "I'm safe; how did you know I needed to talk to you?"

"Thomas woke me up and told me bird girl could use a little help."

"This campground feels so different from all the others; I feel like I wouldn't be safe here at all if Captain X wasn't looking out for me."

"Can you leave tomorrow and spend tomorrow night in Mobile?"

"I don't think so, but I can't exactly say why. I think there's something Captain X wants me to do before I leave." Wren inhaled deeply, but it turned into a wide, genuine yawn. "I think I can go to sleep now."

Justin exhaled. "I can too, now that I know Thomas will wake me if you're in trouble; we'll talk tomorrow."

Wren turned off the lights and climbed into bed.

When she heard three thumps on the roof of the van, she smiled as she rolled over onto her side. "Good night, Cap'n."

Chapter Nine

Rascal whined; Wren opened one eye and peeked at her phone. "It's only five thirty, Rascal, and it's still dark."

Wren covered her head with her pillow, but Rascal whined louder and higher in pitch.

"Okay, boy; we'll go outside." Wren moaned as she climbed out of bed. "I hurt all over."

Rascal stood at the door and whined again.

She yawned as she threw on her jacket over her pajamas and put on a pair of socks and her boots. After she picked up her stick, she stuck her pistol into her jacket pocket; Rascal stared at her.

"You didn't give me time to get dressed; my pistol's too heavy for my pajama bottoms." Wren pulled out her flashlight from her backpack.

"Okay, I'm ready." She opened the door, and they went outside. Rascal barked, and Wren heard a muffled bark in return; Wren watched as April's fifth wheel rounded a corner and headed toward the driveway.

"We came outside to tell Jolie and April safe travels, didn't we? I'm glad we did."

Wren sighed as she stared at the stars that twinkled against the backdrop of the dark sky before she examined the area around the van then turned on her flashlight. After Rascal disappeared into the darkness, she listened to the katydids and tree frogs.

When Rascal reappeared, Wren said, "I'd like to take a shower; maybe that will help my achy muscles."

After she gathered her shower gear, towel, and clean clothes, Wren hobbled to the rest room while Rascal investigated their surroundings as he darted around her.

Rascal lay across the door while Wren showered. When she was dry and dressed, Wren examined her face in the mirror and groaned. "The swelling is mostly gone, but now I have a black eye in addition to a scraped chin, nose, and forehead. It's Florida; I'll wear my sunglasses to hide my eye."

On the way back to her van, Wren smelled the familiar, now-welcome odor that came with Captain X.

"Lassie, the pirate's princess needs help." Captain X blocked her way to the van; he pointed at the office.

Wren turned to glance at the office. "The lights are on, and Taliyah's car is still there. Do you suppose she was up all night packing?"

"Go," he ordered.

Wren changed direction to go to the office. Rascal whined then raced ahead and waited for her on the porch.

"Door's probably locked," Wren mumbled.

"It isn't," Captain X bellowed. "Go inside."

When she joined Rascal, Wren tried the door handle; she raised her eyebrows when the door opened.

"Taliyah?" Wren and Rascal went inside.

Wren heard a moan from the breakroom; she dropped her shower bag, dirty clothes, and stick and raced across the room. She tripped when she reached the doorway; when she grabbed onto the door jamb to keep from falling, Wren twisted her knee.

Taliyah was sprawled on the floor, and her legs were entangled in a broken chair.

"What happened?" Wren limped to Taliyah's side.

Taliyah struggled to get up. "I wanted to take down Dad's handmade sign he put over the doorway, but the chair shook and moved when the earthquake hit and I fell. I think I hit my head, or maybe I drank too much wine because I've been fighting with this ridiculous chair all night."

"Do your legs or your hip hurt?"

"My arm hurts; I think I tried to catch myself when I went down."

Wren slowly and painfully limped to Taliyah before she lowered herself to the floor and exhaled.

"Let me know if I'm hurting you." Wren slowly rotated the chair while she watched Taliyah's face.

Wren stopped when Taliyah gasped then loudly exhaled with a moan before she sharply inhaled.

Taliyah groaned, "Go ahead; I'm okay."

Wren shifted the chair until she was certain Taliyah's legs would clear the rungs. "I think I can remove the chair now."

Taliyah clenched her teeth. "Do it."

Wren carefully slid the chair away from Taliyah.

Taliyah exhaled. "I panicked and kicked the chair, but it wouldn't move, so I kicked again and again until I ended up even more twisted with every kick."

Taliyah raised herself up onto her elbow and heaved on the floor.

Wren gagged at the overwhelmingly foul odor of sour wine. "Don't try to get up, Taliyah; stay where you are. You may have a concussion." Wren dialed nine-one-one.

The dispatcher answered. "The sheriff is on his way, Wren."

"We need an ambulance at the campground. Taliyah fell and may have a concussion."

"Oh, good; it isn't you," the dispatcher said. "One second; okay, the ambulance is on its way too."

Wren made her way to a chair next to the table and sat. "I twisted my knee and dropped my stick at the door."

Tears dripped onto her shirt; Rascal whined and licked her face. Wren put her arm around him and buried her face in his neck while she sniffled.

"I'm so sorry, Wren. I'll let the sheriff know," the dispatcher said.

"It's terrible you got caught in the middle of a power war; stay strong," Taliyah moaned.

"What do you mean, power war?"

Taliyah moaned, "I've said too much; still drunk, or maybe that concussing thing you said." Taliyah gagged then threw up again.

When Taliyah's elbow slipped, she fell onto her back.

"Move over to your side, Taliyah; you don't want to aspirate anything into your lungs."

When Taliyah gurgled with every breath and didn't move, Wren yowled with pain as she made her way to Taliyah and sat on the floor next to her while she grunted then screamed as she pushed with both legs against the woman's heavy body to move her onto her side.

"You make a lot of noise," Taliyah muttered as she rolled.

Wren giggled in between her gasps and sobs of pain. "I do, don't I?"

Rascal rose and trotted to the front door. When he barked, Wren said, "Good boy, Rascal. Tell them where we are."

Rascal howled then barked.

Wren closed her eyes when she heard the sirens. "The ambulance will be here in a minute, Taliyah."

Taliyah gasped, then her breathing became ragged.

"Hang in there, Taliyah."

Taliyah's breathing became more erratic until there was only silence.

"Oh, no," Wren whispered.

"Breathe, Taliyah!" Wren screamed as she pushed Taliyah with her feet.

Taliyah jerked then wheezed.

"Wren!" the sheriff shouted.

Rascal barked; the sheriff appeared in the doorway.

The sheriff knelt next to her. "Wren, are you okay?"

"I twisted my knee; Taliyah needs an ambulance." Wren sobbed. "Somebody needs to help her."

The sheriff gently raised Wren to a sitting position and held her steady. "The ambulance is here."

When the ambulance crew raced inside, the sheriff said, "Wren's okay. Taliyah is your patient."

The ambulance crew swooped up Taliyah onto their stretcher and left.

The deputy rushed into the room as the sheriff asked, "Wren, what happened?"

Wren told them about her visit to the office the night before and what Taliyah said to her when she and Rascal came into the office.

"Did the power war she mentioned make any sense to you?" the sheriff asked.

Wren shook her head. "Not at all."

"What can we do for you, Wren?" the deputy asked.

"Coffee," Wren said. "Maybe ice for my ankle and knee."

The deputy disappeared; the sheriff chuckled. "I'll take you and Rascal to breakfast, and you can get your coffee."

"I'll need my sunglasses."

Sheriff peered at Wren's face and whistled softly. "Yes, you will, and a ball cap."

After the deputy returned with two tea towels, he emptied an ice tray from the small refrigerator in the corner into two plastic sandwich bags and wrapped the bags with the towels. "Two icepacks courtesy of the Lost Pirate Campground."

The sheriff helped Wren to her feet while the deputy pulled a chair close for her to sit. The deputy gave one icepack to Wren for her right knee while he placed the other one against her left ankle.

Wren sighed. "How's Taliyah?" She narrowed her eyes as the sheriff and deputy exchanged glances.

"Taliyah was breathing with the assistance of the ambulance crew when they loaded her into their rig," the sheriff said.

"She must have hit her head when she fell," Wren said. "When I found her, she told me she had lost her balance because of an earthquake."

The sheriff scanned the room. "You said she drank a bottle of wine out of a tumbler?"

Wren nodded. "She emptied the bottle."

"I don't see a used paper cup, a wine bottle, or a tumbler anywhere." The deputy checked the trash can. "It's empty."

"Check around the registration desk while I help Wren to my cruiser," the sheriff said.

When a Florida state trooper came inside the office, the sheriff said, "I won't be long, Wren; will you be okay?"

"If I can have my stick, I can go back to my van and make coffee."

"I'll get your stick and help you back to your van, but I don't think you'll be able to manage with just your stick with your left ankle and now your right knee out of commission," the deputy said. "I'd be happy to drop you off at the café for coffee while I go to the drug store and get you a pair of crutches."

Wren's lower lip quivered. "You're right."

As the deputy practically carried Wren the entire way to her van, he said, "I didn't call the marshal; it's too early in Arizona for a call."

"Yes, it is." Wren pursed her lips to keep from smiling. *Which is exactly why I'm going to call him.*

After Wren and Rascal were inside the van, she washed her hands and changed clothes then called Justin.

"Wren?" Justin's voice was groggy. "What's wrong?"

"I took a shower early this morning; on my way back to my campsite, I noticed the lights were on at the office, and Taliyah's car was still parked near the building."

"What? I'm having trouble following you," Justin said.

"That's too bad; you'll catch up. Taliyah fell off a chair because her balance was wonky after she drank an entire bottle of wine, or maybe the earthquake threw her down."

"Wren, you win. Are you okay?"

"I twisted my knee."

"I'm not following any of this conversation."

"Of course you aren't; my ankle is better, but my knee hurts, and I'm a total wreck. I'll tell the deputy he can call you."

"Wait; you win."

"Naturally; I love you, honey, but I just wanted to wake you up. I'll tell the deputy he can call you because I'm teetering on the edge of hysteria."

"No, I want to hear it from you; tell me your hysterical version."

Wren told him about finding Taliyah, twisting her knee, and what Taliyah said.

"What does Captain X say?"

"You're more alert than you let on or else I talked too long and gave you enough time to wake up. After I took a shower, and Rascal and I were on our way back to the van, Captain X told me the Pirate Princess needed my help. That's when I saw the lights were still on at the office, and Taliyah's car was still parked at the office. The deputy is waiting to take me to a café, so the sheriff can buy me breakfast, and I can have coffee. Can I tell the deputy he can call you?"

Justin snorted. "Please do; love you like crazy, darlin'.'"

"Love you so much." Wren hung up.

Wren opened the van door, and Rascal hopped into the waiting deputy's cruiser.

After the deputy helped her into the cruiser and headed toward the café, she said, "You can call the marshal anytime. I woke him up, so he's waiting to hear from you."

The deputy side-glanced Wren.

"What?" she asked.

"Nothing."

"I don't think I'll need the crutches after all; my knee isn't as painful as it was right after I fell."

"Let me know if you change your mind."

When they reached the edge of town, Wren asked, "Will the café be open?"

"They open at seven; we might be a little early, but they'll let you in and give you coffee."

When the deputy parked at the café, he said, "When I told you it was too early to call Arizona, I knew I was wrong just from your tone of voice when you agreed with me. Wren, it was a little scary."

The deputy opened the back door for Rascal. By the time he and Rascal had rushed around the cruiser to help her, Wren had climbed out of her seat and closed the door; she stood next to the vehicle.

"I think if I can remember to take it slow, I'll be okay, but I wouldn't mind a little help with the steps."

Wren hobbled to the steps and grabbed onto the railing; the deputy put his arm around her waist while he helped her.

When they were on the porch, she exhaled from the exertion. "Thanks; I've got it from here."

He opened the café door for her. "Good, I'll call Justin."

When she went into the café, the server called out, "Hey, Ms. Wren. You and Rascal don't have to sit out on the patio because it's too chilly for me and my Florida blood. Sit wherever you like, and I'll bring you some coffee. Cream and sugar?"

"No, just plain; doesn't even have to be hot." Wren sat at a table that was close to the kitchen.

The server giggled as she brought a glass of ice, a cup, and a pot of coffee to Wren's table. "We had an elderly gentleman who was a regular; he always ordered a small glass of ice with his coffee, so he could cool it down. You want a menu?"

"The sheriff will be here soon; I suppose it would be polite to wait for him to order."

"Gotcha." The server left the two menus she had under her arm, then disappeared.

Wren glanced out the front window at the deputy who wildly gestured with his free hand while he talked on the phone.

"If I didn't have a cup of coffee that was at the perfect temperature, Rascal, I'd go closer to the door to eavesdrop," Wren whispered.

Rascal raised his eyebrows as he pointedly stared at Wren's stick as the sheriff came into the café.

"You don't have to remind me," Wren hissed.

"A state crime scene investigator showed up right after you left, Wren. We were lucky to catch him; he was on his way to go fishing. He and I searched the office and the trash, and he searched the dumpster. We didn't find a wine bottle, a Lost Pirate tumbler, or any paper cups except those that were still in the cupboard and unused."

"I forgot to tell you that Taliyah poured wine into a paper cup for me."

"So, there should have been two cups, right?"

"No, I didn't drink any of the wine, but I didn't want to hurt Taliyah's feelings; I took my cup back to the van with me."

"Did you pour it down your sink?"

Wren furrowed her brow. "I actually don't use my sink. I planned to take it to the restroom to pour down the sink, but I forgot about it; it's next to the van's front tire on the passenger's side."

"I'll be right back." The sheriff strode out of the café and made a call.

"He's not waving his arm like the deputy did, Rascal; doesn't he look awfully smug?" Wren whispered.

Rascal slowly rose from his comfortable napping spot near Wren's feet and moved closer to the front window; he cocked his head and stared at the sheriff. The sheriff frowned when he noticed Rascal and turned his back.

When Rascal returned to Wren, she giggled. "Did you get the impression he didn't want you to read his lips?"

Rascal grinned.

The sheriff's face was tight as he joined Wren and Rascal at the table. "The crime investigator found it right where you said; he's excited to have the evidence that will rule out drugs. Do you know if Taliyah made it a habit to drink heavily?"

"I don't have any idea; she did seem to be a little surprised that the bottle had been opened, and the cork had been replaced, but I thought she was forgetful."

The sheriff picked up his menu. "I'm starving; what about you?"

"Eggs and grits sound perfect; it'll be like home," Wren said.

"Got it; plus your blueberry turnover and a cinnamon roll to go," the server said.

The sheriff frowned at the menu.

"I'll put in your usual, Sheriff." She refilled their coffee before she flitted away to the order window as an elderly couple came inside the café. Before they were seated, the server scribbled on her pad and called out, "Order!" She hurried to their table with a tray that contained coffee cups, two spoons, the coffee pot, and a sugar bowl and creamer.

The sheriff tapped his cap with two fingers in a salute to the elderly gentleman; the man acknowledged the sheriff with a nod.

"That's our retired US Senator; he was always true to his Florida roots and a remarkably skilled negotiator; good man."

The server brought their breakfast. While they ate, the sheriff said, "Wren, I have a little pull, so at the marshal's request, one of the best undercover officers the state has been assigned to the investigate the murders. I don't know what you know, and I don't think you know what you know, but you have to be making the killer nervous."

"Everything I've read says that Eugene Hawthorne's murder is still a cold case and is long forgotten. Is that true, or is someone working on it?"

The sheriff gazed at Wren. "Someone's always poking at the cold cases now and then. Are you thinking it's related to the two murders? How does Taliyah fit in?"

"I don't have a clue."

"Literally?" the sheriff raised his eyebrows.

Wren chuckled. "Literally."

The server brought their cinnamon rolls in a takeout box and cleared their dishes.

"But you have a hunch."

Wren tilted her head. "I don't have hunches; it's more like the pieces fall into place for me."

"You don't have enough pieces, do you?"

"I'm not really sure; I may have the right pieces, but I may be focused on the wrong pieces or don't realize what I have."

When the server brought him the check, the sheriff said, "I may be getting old, but that made sense to me. Let me know how I can help stop this killer."

The sheriff helped Wren to her feet; as Wren slowly made her way to the door with Rascal at her side, the sheriff stayed close as he carried her cinnamon roll.

On the way to the campground, the sky lightened. Wren looked over her shoulder as the sun rose behind her.

"When are you leaving?"

"First thing tomorrow morning," Wren said.

"I'd tell you it would be safer if you left today, but you're probably too tired to be driving most of the day."

Wren smiled when she glanced back at Rascal; the sun that rose behind them cast beams of a halo around Rascal's head.

She yawned. "I didn't get much sleep."

When they went past the campground office on the way to Wren's campsite, Wren's eyes widened. "There's a truck at the office." The sheriff nodded. "The investigator must have what he needs; he told me he'd contact the family when he was finished."

The sheriff helped her out of his cruiser and to the van door; when he handed her the small white sack with her cinnamon roll, he said, "Call me if you need me, but please don't need me."

After Wren and Rascal were in the van, she started a pot of coffee and turned on her laptop. "I have so many questions about Taliyah; why is she Taliyah Simpson instead of Taliyah Hawthorne? Was she married, or was that her mother's last name before she married Eugene?"

After two hours of drinking coffee, munching on her cinnamon roll, and taking notes while she searched the internet, Wren sniffed. "I keep smelling something sour; it's me."

She tentatively rose to her feet with the help of her stick. "So far, so good."

Wren gathered fresh clothes and her shower gear. "I'm not interested in driving all day to Mobile with stinky clothes in the van. We can start a load of laundry after my shower."

Wren stuffed her dirty clothes into a pillowcase and put her clean clothes and shower gear inside her backpack.

On the way to the restroom, she said, "We could even go to the office to see who is there after we get the laundry going; it might be a family member who could clear up my questions about Taliyah."

After her shower, Wren exhaled. "I feel so much better."

She gazed into the mirror at her face. "I forgot my sunglasses. I wonder if I put my spare pair in my backpack."

Wren dug through her backpack and pulled out her spare sunglasses and a large envelope; she peered into the envelope. "I'd forgotten all about the old pictures of the campground Taliyah gave me." She returned the envelope to her backpack before she and Rascal went to the laundry room.

After she started the washer, Wren and Rascal went to the office; when she opened the door, Rascal trotted in, and she followed him.

Crystal stepped out of the breakroom. "I'm glad to see you, Wren. Are you okay?"

"As long as I don't take another fall, I'm fine," Wren said. "I'd forgotten that you were related to Eugene Hawthorne."

"When the family heard Taliyah was in the hospital, one of Dad's brothers called him and asked if I would manage the campground. Dave has good contacts and found a trailer for us to rent, so we'll be staying here for a while; we'll be your neighbors starting this afternoon. Come on in and sit down; I've cleaned the room, but I'm going through Eugene Hawthorne's papers I found in some boxes behind cartons of jarred pickles that were stacked in the closet; he must have been a real packrat. Want to help me take a break?"

"I'd love to; I am so unclear about Taliyah's relationship to Eugene."

"Come sit; that walk from your van must have been exhausting," Crystal said.

As Wren slowly made her way to the table, Crystal hurried to help her.

"After I showered, Rascal and I started a load of laundry, so we actually made our way here in stages," Wren said.

"You're smart. Do you want ice for your knee?"

Chapter Ten

Wren groaned as she sat at the table. "Ice is definitely a good idea."

Crystal put ice into a small baggie then wrapped it with paper towels. After she handed the makeshift icepack to Wren, she pointed to a small white box in the middle of the table. "I bought cookies for inspiration; help yourself."

While they munched on cookies, Crystal said, "You've stumbled onto a family scandal; at least it was almost fifty years ago. Eugene Hawthorne was Taliyah's father, but Dorthea was married to someone else when she got pregnant; his last name was...want to guess?"

"Simpson?"

"Exactly; Mr. Simpson was an abusive drunk, according to the family lore; my grandmother tells this story so much better than I do, by the way." Crystal smiled. "Anyway, Mr. Simpson was the original owner of the Lost Pirate Campground; Eugene Hawthorne managed the marina, and unknown to Simpson, ran an extremely lucrative smuggling operation. Eugene smuggled anything and everything, but he was particularly well-known in the big money circles for smuggling high-quality Cuban rum."

"That makes sense, given the time period; so, in a way, Eugene Hawthorne was the pirate."

Crystal nodded. "Mr. Simpson was found dead on the beach; the official cause of death was natural causes because of an alcohol overdose, but he had quite a crack in his skull that could not have happened when he fell on the sand."

"Do you suppose Eugene Hawthorne was taking care of the family he considered his own?"

"Could be; Dorthea inherited the campground and marina and promptly married Eugene Hawthorne when Taliyah was three, I think. Eugene and Taliyah were very close. Taliyah went by the name Hawthorne until Dorthea divorced Eugene and took the name Simpson, out of spite, according to Granny. Dorthea drained the campground of every penny of profit then some. Can you tell my sweet, frail Granny was not a Dorthea fan?"

"What about the marina?"

"Granny said Dorthea couldn't get her hands on the smuggling money; the legitimate marina ran at a loss, so she didn't want it."

"What about Nadia?"

Crystal raised her eyebrows. "Taliyah told you about Nadia? Nadia wanted nothing to do with the Simpson kid, which is what Granny said Nadia called Taliyah."

"That's terrible."

"Our entire family agrees with you except with much stronger words; Granny was proud to announce that the no-good, nasty Nadia was not related to us. Granny loved alliteration; she always maintained that Nadia murdered Eugene."

"Was Nadia a local? Where is she now?"

"We don't know; she just suddenly appeared then disappeared." Crystal side-glanced at Wren. "Do you have any idea how good you are? You're easy to talk to, and your interrogation has a natural, casual flow to it."

Wren's eyes widened; she whispered, "You're a cop."

Crystal giggled. "That's silly."

Wren smiled. "Of course it is. Thank you for clearing up my confusion about Taliyah. Is she going to be okay?"

"We don't know yet." Crystal peered at Wren. "The wine had a high concentration of ethylene glycol."

Wren snorted. "That's right up my alley: ethylene glycol is an industrial synthetic compound: odorless, colorless, slightly sweet, and highly toxic to humans; the toxins attack the nervous system, heart, and kidney, but alcohol delays the toxicity effects."

Crystal raised her eyebrows. "How did you know that?"

"I wrote an informational article for a school district whose high school students were daring each other to drink antifreeze; unfortunately, it became such a popular fad that the younger ones in middle school were picking it up. The kindergarten teacher was a marketing whiz. She helped me develop age-appropriate campaigns for the two age groups of students and a third campaign for the teachers and parents." Wren's eyes twinkled. "We didn't include the alcohol part."

"Lucky for Taliyah that whoever was trying to poison her didn't know about the alcohol and certainly didn't expect you to have a sample, so her medical team could quickly intervene appropriately. Taliyah will probably be okay, thanks to you."

"Last night, she told me she was leaving in the morning to live with her mother," Wren said.

Crystal frowned. "My uncle told me she hasn't been happy here since her dad died, but if she was planning to leave right away, she must have felt threatened."

"Maybe she did, but I'm positive she sincerely believed this was not the place for her with her dad gone."

"Dave has been campaigning for me to quit my job; we'll see what works out," Crystal said.

"Wouldn't you miss the logistics?" Wren asked.

"I would, but after the renovations are completed, my uncles plan to hire staff to manage it; I could easily find another logistics position or even open my own business."

"What about the marina?" Wren asked.

Crystal's eyes gleamed as a wicked smile spread across her face. "The marina needs a little housekeeping; it's mine."

"Good; we'll help."

"No; absolutely not." Crystal's tone and her face were hard.

Wren rose. "Okey-dokey; let's go check the laundry, Rascal."

Crystal grumbled, "I'll put the clothes into the dryer for you. Have another cookie; I'll be right back."

Crystal rushed out of the room then called out before she left. "Do not go anywhere and leave me two cookies."

When the door slammed, Wren grabbed a cookie, then grimaced as she hobbled with the help of her stick to the registration desk. She sat on the stool and exhaled from the exertion before she pulled out a treat for Rascal then opened the other drawer at the desk.

Rascal stared at her.

"I'm not actually snooping; I'm looking for the library books just in case Taliyah forgot to return them."

Rascal snorted.

While she was checking another drawer, Wren spotted a key in the back of the drawer. When the campground phone rang, she pulled out the key and stuck it into her pocket. On the fourth ring, Wren shrugged as she answered the phone in her best imitation of Betsy's style of campground greeting.

"Avast, matey, it's a treasure of a morning at the Lost Pirate Campground; how can we help you today?"

"I'm calling to see if Wren Weaver is still there."

Wren's nostrils flared. *Blake.*

Wren took a cleansing breath. "I'm sorry, sir, but we're pirates, not spies."

"Can I leave a message for her? It's urgent."

"We don't have any way to deliver messages; if there's nothing else I can do for you, have a clear sailing day."

Wren hung up and laughed as Crystal came inside.

"What's so funny?" Crystal asked.

"Me." She told Crystal about Betsy and how she answered the phone at the Forbidden Oasis Campground.

When Wren told Crystal how she answered and ended the call, Crystal chuckled. "You're right; you're funny."

The phone rang again. Wren glanced at the caller ID. "A former acquaintance who is a jerk, and he's calling back."

"Ah." Crystal pushed the speakerphone button as she answered. "Lost Pirate Campground."

"I just called," Blake said. "I think I was disconnected."

"Sorry for the fall off the plank, mate; what is the date of your arrival?" Crystal winked at Wren, who covered her mouth to stifle her giggle.

"I don't want a reservation; I just wanted to know if Wren Weaver is still there."

"Are you a family member?" Crystal asked.

"Umm...her brother."

"I'm sorry you've missed her, Mr. Weaver; she left early this morning."

"Oh, did she say where she was going?"

"What?" Crystal laughed. "Why would she do that? Pirates never stalk; we only pillage."

"Maybe Uncle Charlie..." Blake mumbled as he hung up.

"That was fun; what's next?" Crystal asked.

"I just remembered I have four library books that I was supposed to give to Taliyah before I left."

Crystal shrugged. "Let's get them; I'll return them tomorrow."

After they were outside, Crystal locked the door. "If you won't disappear, I can run to the equipment shed for the golf cart. Dave told me he plugged it in the last time he was here; I guess Taliyah didn't use it very much because he said the battery was completely run down."

As Crystal sprinted toward the shed, she shouted, "Don't go anywhere without me."

"Do you think the clothes are dry, Rascal?"

He growled.

"You're right; we'll wait for Crystal."

Crystal careened the golf cart around the corner and then slammed on the brakes in front of the office.

"I'm glad Dave told me about this; we can pick up your laundry on the way."

Crystal helped Wren into the golf cart; when they reached the laundry room, Crystal went inside, then returned with Wren's laundry in a small crate. "I didn't see a laundry basket, so I used this crate I found in the supply closet; it was empty except for a small stack of old newspapers; I pulled out the page on top but left the rest, so your clothes wouldn't get dirty." Crystal set the cart in the back of the golf cart, then headed to Wren's van.

When Crystal parked next to the van, Wren said, "I won't be long."

"I'll hand you the crate after you're inside. Why don't you grab your computer and spend the morning with me at the office while I go over the bookkeeping?"

"That's a good idea; maybe I'll get some writing done."

Wren stuck her laptop into the computer bag and set it near the door; after she picked up her backpack, she opened the door where Crystal waited.

"I'll put your two bags in the golf cart; it will be easier for you," Crystal said.

After Wren and Crystal were seated in the golf cart, Crystal asked, "Want to race to the office, Rascal?"

Rascal yipped as he took off at full speed.

"Hold on." Crystal slammed down her foot on the accelerator and chased Rascal. Wren clutched the grab bar, then laughed when Crystal almost caught up with Rascal.

"I'm closing in," Crystal called out in glee.

Rascal zoomed ahead, then turned to wait at the building; he grinned while he panted. Crystal threw up her hands in defeat and slowed to a more casual speed as she continued then parked near the front door.

"Pretty good race, thanks, Rascal."

After they were inside, Wren set up her computer on the table in the breakroom. Crystal gave Wren an icepack for her knee and continued hovering until Wren growled, "Don't you have work to do?"

Crystal stopped to rub Rascal's ears before she flounced out of the room. "Yes, I do, but I was busy procrastinating." Wren opened the draft of her novel; after she read the previous chapter, she began typing and was soon deep into the story.

"Wren?"

Wren jumped at a light touch on her shoulder.

"I didn't mean to startle you, but I need to talk to you," Crystal said. "Dave just called, and he has a flat tire on the trailer. The good news is that he found it when he stopped at a rest area; the bad news is that the spare has dry rot. He's less than an hour away, so I'll pick him up, and we'll buy a new tire. I'll give you a ride back to your van."

"Won't it be hard to find a trailer tire on a Sunday?" Wren asked.

"He doesn't seem to think so, but he's making calls. If he can find one I can pick up on my way, that would be ideal."

When they reached the van, Wren climbed out; Crystal hopped out, then handed Wren her computer bag and her backpack.

"Wait," Crystal said. "Why don't I leave the golf cart with you? You'll have a way to get back and forth to the rest room to give your knee and ankle a rest."

"I appreciate it; my ankle is much better than it was last night, so if I'm careful, my knee should be better tomorrow for the trip to Mobile."

"Here's the key to the golf cart." Crystal handed Wren a keyring. "I added it to the campground keys, so I wouldn't lose it. I'll see you when we get back." Crystal sprinted to the office where she had parked her car.

Wren opened the folder Crystal had given her from the storage closet and took notes as she went through the financial documents. "These numbers don't balance at all; according to the notes in the margin, Eugene Hawthorne audited the campground and recorded the results from his preliminary findings; he would have had access to the original source documents." She read the next few documents. "These are signed by Nadia; Eugene's note on the bottom of the last page says, 'Check figures.'"

"I wonder what made Eugene suspicious in the first place." Wren kept reading. "This goes back farther than I expected."

She opened her laptop. "I wonder if I can find the date that Simpson died."

After a quick search, she found the date. "Ah, ha. Nadia must have stepped in as the bookkeeper for the campground after Simpson's death because that's where Eugene started his audit. I wonder if Eugene suspected Nadia killed Simpson, so she could take over the campground, then the marina."

Wren shuffled through all the papers that had been paper-clipped together. "I finally found copies of a few tax records for the marina signed by Simpson with a question mark and Eugene's initials in the margin. Seems like a motive for Nadia to have wanted to silence Eugene. I wonder if Nadia did the bookkeeping for the marina."

Rascal tilted his head and gazed at Wren.

She sighed. "It's logical, but it's not solid enough without confirmation, is it? Too bad the library's closed today; I need to talk to someone who's been around for a while and would know if Nadia had taken over filing the taxes for the marina, in addition to the campground."

Wren straightened the papers while she was deep in thought. "I have an idea, Rascal. The other box might be the records for the marina. We can zip up there, take a quick peek, and come back."

After they were in the building, Wren locked the door and went to the breakroom to sit next to the box. She pulled out the top paper-clipped set. She flipped through the pages then smiled. "If I look at the top two pages and the last page, I think I can go through the box fairly quickly and pick out potential groups to review more closely. Someone was very organized, Rascal."

Wren stopped and reviewed a year's worth of income and expense sheets for the marina. "Eugene took the conservative approach; the marina was modestly profitable on paper, but the income and expense sheets don't match the tax records that Simpson signed."

Wren replaced all the papers into the box in the order she had found them. "If I had a lucrative smuggling business like Eugene's, this is exactly how I would want my records to be."

Rascal whined; Wren heard the crunch of tires and a car engine as it stopped in front of the office. Wren held onto her stick as she rose then slowly limped toward the loud, persistent knocks at the locked door. She narrowed her eyes at the man at the door as he shifted to pounding with his fist.

Wren stepped back to the breakroom doorway. "It's Blake, Rascal."

She called nine-one-one.

"The sheriff is on his way, Wren. Do you need an ambulance?" the dispatcher asked.

"No ambulance; I'm inside the office at the campground, and the front door is locked. A man I've told to stay away from me is pounding on the door."

"Hold on one second."

While Wren waited, Rascal stepped between her and the front door. "Thanks," she whispered. "He does seem out of control, doesn't he?"

The dispatcher returned. "Wren, you won't hear a siren; I just told the sheriff what you said; he's coming in fast and quiet. Stay on the line with me."

Blake stopped pounding on the door.

Wren stepped out of the breakroom but stayed out of sight.

"Sheriff, I think there's a problem here because no one is answering the door," Blake said.

"The office is closed," the sheriff said.

"Closed? When will they open? I have to leave town," Blake grumbled.

"So, what's stopping you?" the sheriff asked.

Blake cleared his throat. "I have an urgent message for Wren Weaver; her van's here, but she didn't answer her door."

"I'm an old friend of the family; I'll see that she gets the message," the sheriff said.

"It's kind of private."

"Do you want to tell me or move on? You're bordering on loitering here; this is private property."

"I'll call her publisher."

"You do that; we'll be patrolling the campground regularly, not that it matters to you because you don't have any unfinished business here at all, do you?"

Wren smiled when she heard a door slam followed by the crunch of tires on the gravel driveway as a car drove away.

"It's safe now, Wren," the dispatcher said.

When Wren opened the door, the sheriff said, "I don't think he's going to vote for me in the next election. Do you think he's really going to call your publisher?"

"He said he was earlier; I don't know why he hasn't yet, since my publisher is his uncle," Wren said. "Blake and I were friends in college but split up before we graduated."

"And not on good terms, I take it," the sheriff said.

"Not at all."

"I have a kind-hearted friend who would be happy to host you for the night, if you like; she has a cat that gets along with dogs."

Wren smiled. "Dave and Crystal will be here in an hour or so; they'll be staying at the campground, so they'll be close if I have any problems."

After Wren locked the office door, the sheriff stood next to his cruiser while Wren drove the golf cart to her van with Rascal trotting alongside her.

After they were inside, Wren's phone rang. *Charlie; that was fast.*

"Blake has called me twice this morning, Wren; doesn't he have any concept of what time it is in California?" Charlie grumbled. "I'm sorry; I didn't mean to start off complaining. Is now a good time for you to talk? Do you want to call me later?"

"Now's fine." Wren limped to the recliner so she could put up her feet.

"Blake wanted me to tell you he's sorry that the resort articles fell through, but if you were still interested, he was sure he could convince them to reconsider. He said you were really excited about working for him on the new assignment. I heard him wrong, didn't I?"

Wren snorted. "He told me he shared the first two campground articles with a resort, I think in Miami, but he evidently claimed full credit for them. He proposed I write a few articles for the resort, and he would take full credit and all the pay. If it had been anyone besides Blake, I would have laughed at the joke."

"Wren, I probably was the source of the assignment being canceled. The general manager for the Miami resorts called me yesterday and asked reference-type questions; for example, did Blake submit the campground articles on time? I told him you were the sole author of the articles. After the general manager asked a few more questions about Blake, he asked if I had your contact information; of course, I told him no." Charlie chuckled.

Wren rolled her eyes. "Did you tell him to contact Blake?"

"Definitely not; I did mention in passing that Blake knew you long before I did."

Wren smiled as she shook her head. "Maybe all this will cause Blake enough headaches that he'll move on."

"His parents and I would like to see him grow up and take responsibility for himself, but that's enough about dreary Blake. Are you leaving for Mobile in the morning?"

"That's my plan."

"You may have told me, but I've forgotten whether you're going to Georgia or Arizona after you turn in the camper van," Charlie said.

"Arizona." Wren felt her face warm.

"That's what I thought. I understand your truck is ready for you; are you going to drive to Arizona?"

"That's my plan; I have friends along the way where Rascal and I can stay overnight, but I'm still working on the details."

"The CEO wanted me to tell you how much he appreciated the valuable feedback you gave him on the different styles of small campers. He said he won't forget how good-natured you were about each one and plans to make it up to you."

"That was nice of him to say, but I'm not sure how good-natured I was."

Charlie chuckled. "He told me his entire company is aware of your feelings on the topic of composting toilets."

Wren nodded. "I'm completely cured of thinking the tiny trailers are for me."

"If I come up with something I think might interest you, is it okay if I call you? I can promise you Blake would not be included at all."

"That would be fine as long as your feelings wouldn't be hurt if I turned down the offer; I'm not interested in any travel for a while, though."

"Makes sense to me; I have more irons in the fire than just the travel magazine, so something could come up."

After they disconnected, Wren said, "I don't know if Charlie has mellowed or if I've just become used to him."

Wren snorted as she opened her laptop to write. "Anyone would seem normal compared to Blake."

After an hour, her phone buzzed a text from Crystal. "Still looking for a tire. You okay?"

Wren replied, "We're fine."

Wren stared at her phone. "It wouldn't take long for us to get to the bait shop if I take the golf cart; the boardwalk is wide enough for it most of the way."

Rascal growled.

"Don't be so cranky; we'll be fine."

Wren dropped her backpack onto the passenger's seat and used her stick for balance and support while she slid into her seat. "I'll drive as far as I can; if I can't get fairly close to the marina, I'll turn around. Happy?"

Rascal grinned then loped alongside the golf cart. As she neared the restroom, she heard a car as it headed down the driveway.

Wren turned sharply and parked behind the building before she limped back to peek around the corner. "It's the deputy, Rascal; I'll bet he's here to check on me; why do I feel sneaky?"

Rascal yipped.

Wren moved as quickly as she could with her stick and stood next to the restroom door.

"I probably look guilty, don't I?" Wren whispered as she waved at the deputy.

He parked near the building and smiled as he climbed out of his cruiser. "The sheriff asked me to drop by to make sure you didn't have any unwelcome visitors. How are you doing?"

"Much better, as long as I remember to take it slow." Wren returned his smile.

He nodded and continued smiling. "That's good."

Wren nodded and made a slight turn toward the restroom door.

The deputy gazed at his feet then cleared his throat. "Let us know if you're having any problems."

He's not going to leave. "You know I will."

Wren opened the restroom door, and Rascal followed her inside. When she stopped and peered at the mirror, Wren wrinkled her nose. *I look awful; I should have worn my sunglasses.*

Wren pressed her ear against the cool metal door. "I don't hear anything, Rascal, but this heavy door could be muffling sounds. If I peek out, and the deputy sees me, I guess we'll saunter nonchalantly back to the van."

Wren threw open the door, and the deputy's cruiser was nowhere in sight.

Wren exhaled. "Let's ride."

Rascal ran in front of the golf cart as Wren crept along the boardwalk. "It looked much wider when we were on foot, didn't it?"

When she came to the area that was wide, she turned the golf cart around, so it would be facing the campground. "The worst of the uneven and broken boards are ahead. I don't want to take the chance of getting dumped into the swamp. I could never get the golf cart out by myself, and I certainly couldn't explain how it accidentally fell into the mucky water."

As she made her way toward the marina, Wren used the railing and her stick to maintain a steady pace without falling.

Wren and Rascal hurried to the bait shop. The door was closed and had a padlock on a hasp.

"It's locked," Wren mumbled.

The aroma of a freshly squeezed lime tickled her nose but was overpowered by the harsh, sour stink of old fish.

"Locked?" Captain X stood next to her; he threw back his head as he roared with laughter. "That's the oldest trick in the world; look again, lassie."

Wren examined the padlock; its shackle was lined up with the locking mechanism, but not inserted into the body.

"It's not locked." She removed the padlock and hung it on her jeans belt loop, so she wouldn't lose it. She peered inside the bait shop.

"There's the box; they just dropped it on the floor, and a few must have fallen out." She picked up a packet; it was wrapped in brown paper and taped with clear tape. "It's not heavy, Rascal. I'm guessing it's six or so inches long, maybe three inches wide, and about half of an inch thick."

She lifted the lid on the box and peered inside at more of the same-sized packets wrapped in brown paper. "I don't think they'll miss one." Wren stuffed the packet inside the waistband of her jeans. After she put the padlock in the same position that she had found it, she and Rascal hurried back to the golf cart.

She maintained a steady speed on the return trip to the campground. She breathed a sigh of relief when she parked at the van.

After she went inside, Wren carefully slit the tape, then opened the packet.

Her eyes widened; her mouth opened, but it was a few seconds before she could speak. "These are hundred-dollar bills. I just stole a bunch of money; we should put it back, right? Let's go."

Wren's eyes stung, and she coughed at the powerful odor of rotten fish as Captain X blocked the door.

"Ye best stay anchored right here, lassie. No one will miss that packet because the smuggler has won the battle, but not the war. You need to prepare yourself for the war." Captain X disappeared.

"How do I do that?" Wren asked.

"Same way as I do; have some rum and take a nap, lassie."

Chapter Eleven

"That's the best advice or the worst advice I've ever heard. I don't have any rum, but hot tea seems like a reasonable morning substitute." Wren put a coffee cup of water into the microwave to heat.

While Wren sat at the small table and sipped her peach tea, Justin called. "I got a call from the deputy; he told me the sheriff chased off Blake. It sounds like Blake's stalking you, Wren. Keep Rascal close. The deputy and the sheriff are staying close until the new person the state patrol assigned to the case arrives. Do you know who he's talking about?"

"I'm pretty sure I do. I asked Crystal if she was a cop, and she laughed and said that was silly."

"Would I understand if you started at the beginning?"

"Well, I met Dave at the library..."

Justin interrupted as he chuckled. "I did ask for the beginning, didn't I? I'll just take your word for it that Crystal is law enforcement. Do you happen to know which branch?"

"I wouldn't know because she said she wasn't a cop, but my guess is she's a Florida trooper."

"That makes sense. I assume she's investigating the murders and will keep an eye on you because the sheriff and I decided you're somehow a key. What time are you leaving in the morning?"

"I thought we'd leave at first light; it's about a five-hour trip, so we should be there for lunch."

"That sounds perfect. What else do you have going on today?"

"Researching and writing."

"Take it easy. Just in case I forget to tell you later, my phone might be offline a while late tonight or early tomorrow morning, but I'll get back to you as soon as I can," Justin said.

"Be safe; I love you, lawman."

"I love you too, brilliant journalist."

After they hung up, Wren said, "Justin doesn't want me to worry, but I think he'll be tracking someone in the desert tonight. We'll worry anyway, won't we?"

Rascal whined.

"I'll feel better when we're all together too, so we know where he is, what he's doing, and that he's safe."

Wren drummed her fingers on the table while she was lost in thought.

"Let's put the packet somewhere safe," Wren said. "I can put the crate of clothes in the bathroom, and we can put the packet under the clothes. Since Crystal is assigned to the case, whatever it is, we can talk to her about the money when she gets back." Wren frowned. "I'll have to think about that; what if she has to arrest me? I really don't want to delay going to Mobile because that's our first step toward Arizona and Justin."

While Wren put the crate in the tiny bathroom and buried the packet in the middle of her clothes, her phone rang.

"What do I do, Rascal? We're caught," she hissed.

She exhaled in relief as she picked up her phone. *Betsy.*

"Are you doing okay?" Betsy asked. "Because there is something wrong with Justin. He's become really secretive. I asked him if I should make arrangements for a private plane for you and Rascal, and he said no because Rascal gets airsick. Didn't you fly here from Georgia with Rascal? Did you give Rascal some airsick medicine? Can't you get some there for him? Do you need for me to help you with that? I'm not sure exactly what to do, but I can call our vet's office in the morning and ask them."

"That's actually a good idea, except I don't want to leave my truck."

"I forgot all about your truck; I'll send you the itinerary to come here on Interstate 10, which is the quickest way for you to get here from Mobile. You and Rascal are going to get a tent in Mobile, aren't you? I've found the best place for you to stay your first night in Texas. I'll send you the information after we hang up, so you can check it out; let me know if you want me to find an alternative for your first night's stay to be in Louisiana because that would be a shorter drive from Mobile."

"Texas for our first night sounds good."

"I'll send it right away; I can't wait to see you." Betsy hung up.

While Wren sipped the last of her tepid tea, the email from Betsy arrived. Wren opened the document and checked the campground. "Rascal, they have a county dog park close to the campground. You can run off some energy, and I can stretch my legs after the drive. Sounds perfect, doesn't it?"

Wren frowned at another new email from Blake with the subject line, "Offer might still be open." She marked it as spam.

When she finished her tea, Wren said, "Captain X said rum and a nap; I don't think I could nap, but it wouldn't hurt for me to stretch out and rest, would it?"

Wren lowered the blinds and locked her door. When she stretched out on her bed, Rascal laid on the floor next to her.

Wren closed her eyes and exhaled as she thought about Nadia. She suddenly sat up. "Rascal, I've been so focused on Nadia as the murderer and the head of the smuggling, but I don't even know what she looks like. I could be standing behind her in the grocery line, and I wouldn't know it."

Wren rose and grabbed her stick. "I want to pace like Justin does when he's thinking, but that's a bad idea, isn't it?"

Wren raised the blinds and stared out across the campground. "When those two men moved their cargo from the marina, they went on a path. Where does it go? There has to be a road or a building close enough for them to walk to and return to the marina before daylight. I'm going to pull up a map online and see what I can find."

A few minutes later, Wren leaned back in her chair. "There's a road on the other side of the marina less than a mile away. If that was where the two men took their cargo, I can see why they wanted to take everything in one trip. I think there must be a roadside picnic area because I saw a cleared section that must be parking; it looked like there was plenty of room for a large truck to pull in, but there wasn't enough room for anything other than a car to turn around. The woods are thick between the marina and the road in the satellite view, so I couldn't tell if there is a path, but there must be."

Wren examined the satellite view more closely. "Just because I can't see it doesn't mean it isn't there. I'd really like to see if that area I think is parking shows any signs of regular use, but the only way to get there is to drive. Our bright yellow camper van is too conspicuous, and the golf cart would be too, in addition to not being legal to travel on a public road."

Wren's phone rang. When she answered, Crystal said, "Are you doing okay?"

"Just fine; Rascal and I napped for a while."

"That's great that you're resting. This has been such an ordeal; we finally found a place that was open and had the right size tire. We're on our way back to the trailer now, so it will be at least another hour before we return. Did the deputy come by?"

"He did a little earlier."

"That's good; I heard at the gas station before I left he was assigned to help with a manhunt in an adjoining county, so I was worried he didn't have time to run out to the campground. I have news about Taliyah because my family has kept in touch with her doctors. She's holding her own so far, thanks to you; I thought you'd like to know."

"I appreciate it."

Crystal continued, "We're hoping to be back before lunch. I don't expect any new arrivals at the campground until closer to four, so that's one less worry, and the guests who don't register in advance rarely show up before five, according to the records."

After Crystal hung up, Wren grumbled, "We're without supervision for at least an hour, but what good does it do us? I can't walk halfway to the marina after we get as far as we can with the golf cart, then follow that up with a walk that will be who knows how long while we try to find our way to the road on the other side of the woods. Even if I could, I'd still have to make the same trip back; I'm certain my knee isn't ready for that much strain."

Wren inhaled. "I channeled my inner Betsy for a minute there, didn't I? I need fresh air; maybe a short walk or a ride around the campground will get rid of my excess energy."

Wren dropped her backpack on the passenger seat of the golf cart and waited while Rascal wandered around their campsite.

"My ankle is back to normal, and my knee isn't as touchy as it has been. I might be okay tomorrow except for my black eye and abrasions on my face. I'm glad I have a few days to heal before we're in Arizona; Justin would have a fit if he saw me, wouldn't he?" Wren chuckled. "Not to mention Betsy."

She scanned the empty campground. "The campground will be different after the improvements, won't it?" She furrowed her brow as she stared at the office. "Taliyah's car is still here, and it's not bright yellow; that gives me an idea. Let's go to the office, Rascal."

Wren unlocked the office door and went inside. "Taliyah said I could use her car to go into town, so I'm sure she wouldn't mind if we take a quick ride just around the corner to the next road, Rascal; besides, we might learn who tried to poison her."

Wren removed the keyring from its hook on the back of the registration desk.

After Rascal was in the back seat, and Wren had started the engine, she pulled out her phone and stared at the map one more time.

"Okay, I've got it." Wren fastened her seatbelt and headed toward the driveway.

After Wren turned at the end of the driveway and headed down the road, she grumbled, "How can people drive cars? I feel like I'm sitting on the asphalt."

Rascal moaned.

"What are you complaining about? I can't see nearly as far down the road as I could in the van or my truck because we're so close to the ground."

Wren slowed and leaned forward to peer at the road. "I think this is our first turn on the right."

After her next turn onto the road where the roadside park was, her eyes widened, and she shuddered. "Did you see that, Rascal? There was an alligator in that ditch. I'm really glad we decided against walking through the woods because I'd completely forgotten about alligators."

When they came to a sign, 'Roadside Park Ahead', Wren slowed, then turned.

She drove past a wooden picnic table with splintered boards and parked near the trees at a spot that couldn't be seen from the wide entry road. "Not a very inviting spot to have a picnic, is it? Its only saving grace is it's surrounded by shade trees."

After Wren climbed out of the car, she stopped. "Rascal, there are sand spurs everywhere; you'll have to stay in the car. I'll just do a quick check, then we'll leave."

Rascal whined, so she lowered all the windows before she closed the door.

Wren watched her steps as she walked back to the dirt road. She continued walking on the wide dirt road until she came to a large open area with a tall, metal building the size of a double car garage near the brush and trees at the far end of the cleared space. She snapped a photo of the building. *This is new; it didn't show on the satellite view.*

When she reached the building, she smiled at the padlock on the door. *It's set up to look locked, just like the bait shop at the marina.*

Wren removed the padlock and peered inside; boxes that were exactly like the box she saw at the bait shop were stacked against the back wall. When she heard the roar of a truck as it turned at the entrance, she snapped a quick photo, closed the door, replaced the padlock in its same deceptive position that she found it, and darted into the woods as a large transport truck pulled close to the building. After the passenger climbed out of the truck, he threw open the wide roll-up door, and the driver backed the truck into the building.

Wren stayed hidden as she returned to the picnic parking area through the woods alongside the road.

She stopped next to the car and listened but heard only birds and the chatter of squirrels.

She turned the car around; after she reached the dirt road, Wren sped to the campground.

As she parked Taliyah's car where she had found it, Wren said, "Now we know where the men took their cargo and what the cargo was, but I'm not sure why the building isn't locked."

Rascal yipped. "That's not really important, is it? What is important is who is the big boss?"

Wren returned the keys to their hook then locked the office door.

As she drove the golf cart back to the van, Wren said, "I need to talk to Justin, but he's busy. I'd call his office and talk to his senior deputy, but it's Sunday, and the sheriff and the deputy here are busy with the manhunt."

After they were inside the van, Wren said, "I could call Cody in Arizona; he's a lawyer, but Justin doesn't trust him because of an old grudge or something between them. I'll call Dad. He doesn't practice criminal law, but I'm sure he must have contacts. Actually, Mom probably does too; I'll call her."

Wren picked up her phone. "No, she'd probably call Justin's mom, and Ellie would call Justin, but he's busy." Wren rolled her eyes. "There I go again: sounding like Betsy. I'll call her; she'll take my mind off my dilemma."

When Betsy answered, she said, "I was just getting ready to call you. Is that why you called me? Everybody here is suddenly unavailable. I need a hobby, so I can be unavailable too. What do you think would be the best hobby for me? I mean, besides reading everything you write. I thought about gardening, but I have the cactus, and that's plenty. There's a beginner's yoga class starting up next week, but I don't look good in yoga pants. What do you think?"

"You'd look great in yoga pants."

"I appreciate the kind words, but my dad always told me to trust but verify; I checked the mirror." Betsy sighed. "Maybe

I should find something to do, so I'll be too busy just like everybody else."

"What about a book club?"

"I hadn't thought of that; I'll check with the library tomorrow to see if there is one I could join."

"If not, maybe you'd like to start one up; you're very organized. You could always say you were busy with your book club any time you like."

"Exactly; I need to go now. I have a thing with my book club. How was that?"

"Very convincing; I expected you to follow up with goodbye."

Betsy giggled. "Thank you."

The tone of her voice turned somber, with a bit of underlying panic. "Will I have to do rules and stuff? What about choosing the books? Will I have to do that too?"

"I'm sure the library has guidelines, and I think most groups vote on the books they want to read."

Betsy exhaled. "You're right; sometimes I get worked up over a problem that never pops up."

"If it's any consolation, so do I, but we get over it, don't we?" Wren asked.

"Problems don't bother you, Wren, but thanks for being supportive. I need to find Butch and tell him I'm too busy to make his sandwich because I have to organize my book club."

"I think it's okay if you make Butch's lunch," Wren said.

"You're right, but I'll tell him I'm too busy to make cookies." Betsy hung up.

"Betsy said something interesting, Rascal, 'trust but verify'. I just realized I had assumed Crystal was the undercover trooper investigating the murders, but we don't really know that for sure, do we? What if she's involved with the smuggling operation? I'm sure she isn't, but I have to verify that she's law enforcement before I say anything." Wren groaned. "How do I do that?"

Wren opened her laptop and searched for Crystal on social media. After half an hour of scouring the internet, Wren said, "I found Dave all over the place but not Crystal. I thought everyone was on social media. I wonder if she uses her maiden name, except I don't know what it is unless it's Hawthorne."

After another hour of following threads that had nothing to do with Crystal or the Hawthornes, Wren closed her laptop and sighed when her phone rang.

"We're fifteen minutes away, Wren. Have you had lunch?" Crystal asked.

"No, I got involved in writing and research and lost track of time."

"We picked up subs and cookies at a sandwich shop when we refueled at a truck stop. They're huge, so I thought you and I could split one. Dave's starving, so we'll eat at the picnic table before we set up."

"That sounds good; I completely forgot about lunch."

After she hung up, Wren and Rascal went outside and watched for Dave and Crystal.

Before Wren saw Dave's truck, she heard the clatter and rumble of the long trailer as it lumbered down the driveway from the road to the campground. After Dave parked at a nearby campsite, Rascal dashed to their truck, and Wren followed him at a measured pace.

"What a day." Crystal set two white sacks on the picnic table while Dave set a six pack of bottles of water next to the sacks. "I ran inside the store and grabbed two daily specials and a dozen freshly baked cookies." She snorted. "I don't even know what the sandwiches are. If we hate them, we'll have white chocolate and macadamia nut cookies for lunch."

Crystal pulled out the sandwiches and a handful of napkins from the larger sack while Dave handed Wren a bottle of water then set one in front of Crystal.

Dave examined his sandwich. "Chicken, avocado, onion, lettuce, tomato, and some kind of spicy mayo; I'd name them the kitchen sink special." He took a large bite and nodded. "Mmm."

Crystal handed Wren a half of the foot long sandwich, and the two of them bit into theirs.

Before Dave took a second bite, he said, "Good choice, honey."

Crystal smiled. "You're easy to please when you're starving."

After Dave polished off his sandwich and water, he rose, then brushed away the clinging bread crumbs from his jeans.

"If you'll unhitch the truck and level the trailer, honey, I'll take care of connecting the utilities," Crystal said.

"Appreciate it. I didn't expect picking up the trailer to take as much time as it did; I've got a meeting with a board in Tallahassee in the morning and still have to collect the additional documentation they will suddenly decide they absolutely must have before they'll approve my proposal. With as much time as I've lost, I'll be working all night."

"Let's get the trailer situated and go home, so you can work and won't lose any more time," Crystal said.

While Crystal connected the sewer line, Wren plugged the electrical cord into the outlet and connected the water hose to the campsite faucet.

"Wren, I'm not sure we'll be staying here tonight; it depends on how comfortable Dave is with his presentation. I'm going to help him as much as I can because if I'm not there to convince him he doesn't need to tweak it for the tenth time, he would stay up all night, then be a wreck in the morning." Crystal narrowed her eyes. "I assume you have a way to protect yourself, do you?"

"Of course, I do; Rascal's very protective."

Crystal nodded. "What about personal protection?"

"I'm not sure what you mean." Wren furrowed her brow as she tilted her head. "Like pepper spray or something?"

Crystal blinked. "Yes, like pepper spray."

"Dad didn't believe in it; he said a bad guy could easily snatch it from me then use it against me."

Crystal nodded. "He's probably right."

"What about you? Do you carry pepper spray?" Wren asked.

"You know, maybe you should go home with us; you'll be safer."

Wren side-glanced at Crystal. *That was an abrupt change of subject.*

"Rascal and I plan to be on the road long before daylight tomorrow; we'll be fine." Wren nodded toward Dave, who was pacing. "He's really stressed, isn't he? Rascal and I need to pack because I'll be turning in the van at the dealership, so we can head toward Arizona. I'll probably turn in early tonight because I'd like to spend tomorrow night in Texas."

"You'll be spending a lot of time behind the wheel tomorrow." Crystal furrowed her brow.

"I like to make the first day of travel the longest because after that, I'm tired of the traffic."

"Evidently, my latest hobby is to worry about everything." Crystal sighed as she glanced at Dave. "You're right about him; let me know if you change your mind or would like to have a home cooked meal with us."

Wren smiled. "Thanks, I will."

After Crystal and Dave left, Wren said, "I still don't know if Crystal is the undercover state trooper, but so what if she isn't? Maybe she's a worrier, just like she said."

After they returned to the van, Wren's phone rang; she grinned as she pulled out the phone from her back pocket. "It's probably Justin."

When she looked at her phone, she sighed, then forced herself to smile as she answered, so she wouldn't sound disappointed.

"I couldn't think of a good reason to call you, so I guess I'm just checking up on you," Kendra said. "I think I read somewhere that's important for a talented editor who is nosy to do. Is your ankle okay, or is that old news? What about your plans for going back to Arizona? Will you be swinging by here, or are we too far out of the way?"

Wren's smile broadened. "My ankle would be old news if I hadn't twisted it again, but it's finally healing. I'm planning to pick up a tent in Mobile, so Rascal and I can camp. I'm afraid Dry Creek, Texas, is too far out of our way."

"That's too bad; I'm sorry we won't see you on your way back. I couldn't think of any other way for you to return to Arizona other than camping, so I researched different styles of tents and showed them to Gage for his opinion. He wasn't impressed at all; he pointed out that any tent with room enough for you and Rascal to sleep comfortably would require two people to set it up. Gage said you'd be better off staying in campground cabins; we can make sure Rascal is welcome wherever you stay."

"I didn't think dogs were allowed in cabins."

"According to Gage, campground owners have discovered that people with dogs will pay a little extra for a dog-friendly cabin that is sanitized between guests and are setting aside one or two cabins for campers with pets. He'd be tickled if he could help you out."

"That would be incredible. Betsy sent me a route with campgrounds; I'll send it to you."

"That would work; if we run into any hiccups, I'll check with Betsy because I'm sure she has already checked for alternates. We'll just make sure you have a safe, comfortable place to stay your first night, then go from there."

Wren sniffled as her eyes welled up. "I really appreciate it; things have been so hectic around here that I haven't really thought beyond leaving first thing in the morning and returning the van."

"That's not you, Wren? What's wrong?"

After Wren told Kendra about finding the two men, then Taliyah, Kendra said, "I am so glad I called you; is there anyone there you can trust?"

Wren exhaled. "Maybe."

She told Kendra about the sheriff, the deputy, the undercover investigator, and Crystal.

"Let me put Gage on that; he'll get us answers," Kendra said.

"But it's Sunday." Wren bit her lip at the quiver in her voice; Rascal put his chin on the back of her hand.

Wren smiled as she stroked his face and exhaled.

Kendra chuckled. "He'll take that as a challenge. What else can we do for you? Walt's going to be peevish because he will be the only one in our family who doesn't have an assignment."

Wren furrowed her brow. *I'd like to know if Justin is okay.*

"That's it," Wren said.

"If you think of anything, call me; I'll talk to you later."

After she hung up, Wren exhaled. "I might as well tough it out and climb the ladder to gather my clothes from the loft."

Chapter Twelve

Wren pulled out her oversized duffel bag and dumped the crate of clean clothes into it before she climbed the ladder. When she was at the top of the ladder, Wren looked at the floor below her. "There's no way I could go down this ladder while I carry clothes, then climb up again for another armload. Rascal, get back by the bed because I'm going to toss everything to the floor, and I don't want to drop them on you."

Wren sat on the loft mattress while she threw clothes over the edge. After she cleared the loft of clothes, she avoided putting too much weight on her right leg as she held onto the rungs.

When she reached the floor, she pulled down the ladder and secured it on the wall with the brackets.

She put her hands on her hips as she surveyed the clothes scattered across the floor. "I have more clothes than I thought; I'll roll them to make them all fit."

Wren carefully rolled each item then put it into her duffel bag. After she finished neatly rolling the last shirt, she collapsed on the bed and moaned as she stretched her back.

"I want to call Justin, but I'd be sad if my call rolled over to voicemail and worried that I was bothering him if he answered. Let's go for a walk along the beach."

As they headed toward the beach, Wren said, "I should have put on shorts; this afternoon has turned really warm."

When they reached the beach, the tide was going out. While Rascal ran with the sanderlings and chased the tide, Wren inhaled the salty Gulf air and gazed at the puffy clouds that looked like floating pieces of cotton that were resting on an invisible flat surface.

"Purdy clouds are liars." Captain X stood next to Wren, and she caught a whiff of fresh fish and pungent lime. "Never turn your back on something that's not quite right."

"What's not..."

Captain X disappeared before Wren finished her sentence.

"...quite right?" Wren squinted at a cloud that was taller than the others. "Weren't all the clouds the same size a few minutes ago?"

Rascal dashed back to Wren and yipped before he ran back to run with the sanderlings.

Wren watched the tide as it receded then sighed. "Come on, Rascal; let's go back to the van."

As she trudged through the sand in the heat, Wren said, "I thought the beach would be relaxing, but now I'm more on edge and overheated. I don't understand what Captain X was talking about, but it certainly sounded like a warning to me. Why can't ghosts be less obscure and just tell me straight out what they're trying to say?"

"The scoundrel has you in their sights, Pirate Girl," Captain X roared. "Load yer cannons, lassie."

"Okay, I get it; I'll be ready," Wren said.

As she continued to her van, Wren mumbled, "Load my cannons."

When she reached her campsite, Wren said, "Captain X, the scoundrel may not know I have cannons."

"Now, you're thinking like a pirate, lassie. Proud of ya!" Captain X roared with laughter.

"At least he quit hollering at me," Wren whispered.

Rascal grinned.

After they were inside, Wren said, "I wish I could talk to Justin."

Wren's eyes twinkled as she sent a text to Justin. "Captain X said I should load my cannons."

Justin replied, "I agree."

Wren's phone rang; she grinned as she answered.

"Honey, I just have a second or two; can you explain?" Justin's voice was muffled.

"Not in a second or two; I needed to hear your voice, so I would know you were okay."

"I'm okay, and I'll see you soon. Load your cannons, sweetheart."

"Will do. I love you; thanks for calling."

"Love you too." Justin hung up.

Wren patted her waistband. "I have my pistol, so I have my cannon loaded, but what is it that's not right, so I won't turn my back on it?"

Wren held her breath while she listened to Rascal breathe. *Captain X didn't take the bait.*

After a few minutes, she said, "Fine, we're on our own, Rascal. I'm going to write."

Rascal closed his eyes while Wren dove into her story.

After two hours, Wren exhaled. "That was a blitz of words, wasn't it?"

She read what she'd written and moved two paragraphs. "That's better."

Wren put her laptop inside the computer bag then glanced around the van. "I have everything packed except for the coffee pot."

After Wren fed Rascal and made herself a sandwich, she opened a bottle of water and took her food outside to sit at the picnic table. "It's not just hot, it's humid. We won't stay outside for very long."

While she ate, she glanced at the sky and frowned. "Didn't Captain X say that pretty clouds were liars? Some of the fluffy white clouds are towering now and have become dark around the edges."

Wren's eyes widened, and she flinched. "That was cloud to cloud lightning; we might see a thunderstorm later this evening."

Wren's phone buzzed to announce a text. "It's Gage, Rascal."

She smiled as she read the text. "C LEO."

"Rascal, Gage said that Crystal is a Law Enforcement Officer. If anyone sees it, they'd think his text said Cleo."

Wren called Gage. "That was really fast, Gage. How did you confirm C so quickly?"

Gage chuckled. "I have contacts. Mom said it was important; are you okay?"

"Yes, and now that I know about Cleo, I feel much better."

"Okay, but it's important that you don't do or say anything that implies what you know about Cleo, especially to her, because you'll put my source in jeopardy."

"Got it, Gage. Trust but verify; I appreciate the verify."

"Glad I could help."

After they hung up, Wren exhaled and gazed at Rascal who was curled up on his favorite rug. "Rascal, we can trust Crystal. She's been elusive because she's undercover; we don't want to blow that, so we'll be cool."

Rascal snuffled in his sleep.

Wren gathered her trash and tied the trash sack. When she opened the door, Rascal stretched, then slowly rose to his feet.

"Are you going with me to the dumpster?"

As the two of them made their way to the dumpster near the driveway exit sign, Wren frowned at the darkening sky. "We may have a rainstorm headed our way. I guess the fluffy clouds were more ominous than I realized."

Wren scanned the campground on her way back from the dumpster. "There are only two campsites occupied: ours and Crystal's. I'll bet the threat of a storm has scared off people."

Before she reached her campsite, large raindrops slammed onto the ground. Wren hurried back to her van. "This is definitely a fast-moving rainstorm; I should have taken the golf cart."

Captain X stood on top of her van with his arms crossed. His voice boomed. "Your purdy clouds are churning, lassie, and a fierce storm hides behind them. It's time for you to abandon ship. Grab your gear and take shelter in that sturdy safe harbor; take dog with you."

Rascal waited while Wren threw on her sweatshirt, snatched up her pillow and blanket from her bed, grabbed her duffel bag and her two bags, and tossed everything into the golf cart; she sped behind Rascal as he raced to the restroom.

While she opened the door, Rascal rushed inside, and her phone rang. Wren pitched all her items from the golf cart into the restroom and closed the door before she answered.

"Wren, we're about to get hit by a dangerous storm; I'm coming to get you," Crystal said.

"Don't do it; I've been watching the sky, and the storm is moving faster than you think. Rascal and I are in the restroom; we'll be safe here. It's too dangerous for you to be on the road."

Crystal groaned. "That's what Dave said. It's a sturdy building, so I guess it's okay if I stay put and be there after the storm passes. Don't leave it until I get there."

After they hung up, Wren grumbled, "Crystal is really bossy; where does she think I'd go?"

She dragged her heavy duffel bag with her computer bag and the backpack on top of it to the farthest corner from the door and the high, small windows that were over the sinks. She folded her blanket and sat on the pad while she leaned against the wall with her pillow behind her.

When the whooshing sound of the wind gusts changed to constant, roaring waves, Wren pulled out her gun range earplugs from her backpack and pulled up the hood of her sweatshirt to cover her ears. Rascal snuggled next to her, and she wrapped her arms around his neck.

The deafening howl of the wind gusts competed with the constant, thunderous roar of the wind. The overhead lights briefly flickered before the restroom was suddenly plunged into darkness.

Wren fumbled in her backpack. "Where's my flashlight?"

When she found it, she turned it on, but immediately turned the light off and shuddered. "Shadows are too creepy."

Wren peered at her phone. "No bars."

The building groaned from the stress of the wind; the rain pounded the roof and sounded like rocks being thrown down from the sky. She closed her eyes and hugged Rascal.

"It's just so noisy," she muttered.

Rascal whined and leaned against her as the sound of the wind continued to grow in intensity until it sounded like a passing freight train. Wren cringed at the pressure against her eardrums and held onto Rascal even tighter.

Rascal whimpered, and Wren stroked him with a shaking hand; she bit her lip to keep from screaming.

A large object slammed against the door with a loud crash; Wren screamed.

"Over here, lassie," Captain X shouted. "Now!"

Wren stared at the shimmering form that stood in the darkness near the first stall then grabbed onto Rascal's collar.

Rascal pulled her into the stall as the roof caved in where they had been sitting.

"Good job, dog," Captain X said.

The spray of the driving rain through the roof drenched Wren and Rascal; Wren shivered, and her hands shook as she pulled her hood back on top of her head.

As the rain slowed, and the wind moved on, Wren exhaled.

"Grab your things, lassie, to get them out of that puddle; your only way out of here is through a window, but there's no hurry," Captain X said.

Wren gaped at the tree that had come through the roof and landed near where she had been sitting. "Is my van okay?" Wren asked.

Captain X disappeared.

Wren turned on her flashlight and pointed it at the ceiling when she set it on the floor. She dragged the duffel bag, computer bag, and backpack across the floor and close to the sinks where it was dry. Her blanket and pillow were soaked, but she draped the blanket over a stall door and put the pillow in a sink to drip.

She rummaged around in the duffel bag until she found a towel. After she rubbed down Rascal to dry him, Wren used the towel to dry her hair.

She shivered in the bone-chilling dampness of her clothes. "Both of us smell like a wet dog, now, but it's too cold to sit around soaked."

Wren stripped and dried herself as well as she could with the damp towel then pulled out a shirt, jeans, socks, and a second sweatshirt and dressed in the dry clothes.

"I feel better." Wren exhaled as she looked at her phone. "I'll try sending a text to Crystal." She tapped a quick text then frowned. "That failed."

Wren frowned at the narrow windows over the sinks. "I don't see how we can get out through those windows; I'm not tall enough to reach them unless I climb up on a sink, and I know I couldn't lift you up, so you could get out."

Rascal trotted to the far end of the room and yipped. Wren picked up the flashlight and shined it on the wall where Rascal stood. "I had completely forgotten about that window with the frosted glass."

She shuddered. "I didn't expect it to be dark outside; I lost track of time."

Wren moved closer to the window; its bottom edge was at her eye level. "It's double-pane glass; I was hoping it was older. I don't think I have anything to break it; maybe there's something in the storage closet I could use."

When Wren tried to open the door, she groaned. "I should have realized it would be locked."

She examined the door handle, then slumped against the door. "I can't remove the plate around the handle because there aren't any screws on this side, and I don't know how to pick a lock."

She sighed as she patted her waistband holster. "Shooting open a lock works in the movies, but not in real life."

Wren rolled her eyes when she touched her pocket. "We might have a solution."

She pulled out the keyring from her pocket. "I must have automatically pulled out the golfcart key when I stopped and stuck the keyring into my pocket before we came into the restroom."

She began trying different keys in the lock; the fourth one unlocked the door. When she opened it, Wren rubbed her hands together. "Let's see what's in here."

She found a push broom, a large carton of folded paper towels, a box of twelve-inch square floor tiles, and a tool chest with a claw hammer inside. She put on her ball cap and pulled up her hood over her cap and tied her hood tightly under her chin. After Wren stuck her sunglasses into her pocket, she grabbed the wet towel.

Wren returned to the window. "Rascal, go back to our stall because there might be some flying glass."

Wren wrapped her hand with the towel, put on her sunglasses for eye protection, and kept her head down as she swung the claw side of the hammer at the bottom corner of the window. The hammer bounced back.

She growled, "This has to work; I just need to use more force."

Wren repeatedly slammed the claw into the corner of the glass until the hammer finally broke through and left a small hole in the glass.

She leaned against the wall and exhaled. "I'll rest just for a minute."

She slid down the wall and closed her eyes. When Rascal nudged her, she was startled. "I fell asleep; I guess I'm exhausted from the stress."

Wren exhaled as she pulled herself up with the help of her stick; she narrowed her eyes at the window. "I'm not playing anymore; you're going down."

Wren broke the glass next to the hole and continued to knock out pieces of glass until almost a third of the window was open to the outside. She grabbed the push broom and slammed the head of the broom against the remaining glass to knock it away from the sill.

Wren folded her blanket over the windowsill then stood on the tool box. After she dropped the floor tiles one at a time out the window, Wren tossed out her stick and wet clothes. She dumped the paper towels on the floor and flattened the large carton then dropped it on top of the clothes and floor tiles.

Wren heaved her duffel bag over the ledge and out the window. After she set her computer bag aside, she lobbed her backpack outside; when it landed with a thud, she stuck the flashlight into the computer bag and slipped the straps over her shoulders.

"Here's my plan, Rascal; I'll climb out and make sure there's no exposed glass, then you can jump out. What do you think? Can you do it?"

Rascal yipped and grinned.

Wren stood on the toolbox then grabbed hold of the bottom of the sill. She simultaneously jumped and pulled herself up; Wren knocked the breath out of herself when she landed halfway across the sill on her stomach. She moaned as she inhaled with a catch of pain.

She carefully exhaled. "I think I bruised a rib."

After she straddled the sill, she maneuvered herself to a sitting position facing out and jumped down to land on the cardboard box, but the cardboard slipped, and she fell. Wren threw out her hands to steady herself as she slid onto the wet sand.

She breathed in relief as she gazed at the stars. "Clouds are gone, Rascal."

She grabbed her stick and climbed to her feet with its help. "Stay right there," she called out. "I need to clear off the glass from the cardboard."

After Wren flipped over the cardboard, then flipped it back, she was satisfied Rascal wouldn't be cut. She placed the cardboard under the window and stood at the side of the window on the cardboard to keep it steady. "Okay, Rascal."

In one smooth motion, Rascal leaped to the ledge then jumped out and joined Wren.

Wren buried her face in his neck. "Good boy."

She picked up her clothes and carefully shook them out then piled them in the sand away from any glass.

She checked her phone. "I have a text from Crystal from half an hour ago; she wants me to call her."

Crystal answered the phone on the first ring. "Are you okay, Wren?"

Wren glanced at her bleeding hands. "We're fine; I haven't checked the campground for damage yet. Rascal and I had to break the window in the restroom to get out."

"We got a call from a neighbor who lost most of their roof. We're going to their place to help put up a tarp and do a little clean up."

"I'll look around and call you back."

"No, don't do that; there might be live power lines down."

"Crystal, there's one line to the main building from the road; the rest of the electrical is underground. I'll call you later."

After she hung up, Wren said, "Crystal is definitely a worrywart."

Wren picked her way around debris as she and Rascal headed toward the front of the building to see what blocked the door. When she flashed her light on the building, her eyes widened at their camping van that was on its roof and crushed against the door. Wren felt her head spin and darkness close in on her; she dropped to her knees and lowered her head to keep from fainting.

While she held her head with her hands, Rascal whined and licked her ear and her cheek. Wren inhaled then slowly exhaled.

After a few more slow breaths, Wren leaned back on her heels. "I guess I thought a window might be broken in the van, but I didn't expect to see it smashed like this."

Wren scanned the nearby campsites with her flashlight, but she didn't see Crystal's trailer.

"Let's check the registration building, Rascal." As Wren held onto her stick with one hand and the flashlight in the other, she carefully followed Rascal to registration.

When they reached the office, Wren shook her head in disbelief. "Can you believe it? This old building looked like it would have fallen apart in a light breeze, but it's still standing."

Wren stepped back to check the roof. "Even the old blue tarp is intact. If there was a tornado behind that rainstorm like Captain X said, it completely skipped this old building."

Wren pulled out the keyring from her pocket. "At least we have a place where we can be comfortable until Crystal comes to pick us up."

After she unlocked the door, she listened. "The silence is eerie; I had hoped the office would have power, but I guess nobody does. Let's get my duffle bag and my other backpack and bring them here; then I'll call Crystal and text Justin."

Wren set her computer bag next to the registration desk before she and Rascal left for the restrooms. She used her stick for balance and her flashlight to avoid tripping over any debris. "This might be the Lost Pirate Campground, but if I'm the pirate Captain X said I am, I'm the pirate on the permanently injured list."

Chapter Thirteen

When they reached the restroom window, Wren leaned her stick against the building wall, then pulled down her blanket and rolled her wet clothes inside it. She slipped her backpack over her shoulders and picked up her duffel bag and put the strap over her right shoulder. "I have to figure out a way to carry the blanket and manage my stick and the flashlight because I'm like the smuggler: I'm not interested in a second trip."

She set the duffel bag on the ground before she put the rolled bundle under her left arm and picked up her flashlight with her left hand. "So far, so good; this next part will be a little tricky, but I think I can do it."

She pulled the duffel bag onto her right shoulder and grabbed her stick. "Let's roll, Rascal."

Rascal led Wren to the office. She dropped the bundle of clothes on the porch before they went inside.

Wren selected a sleeping bag from the shelf and folded it for a comfortable seat. When she called Crystal, it rolled over to voice mail. Wren hung up then sent a text to Crystal. "Call when you can."

She texted Justin. "Severe storm; We're okay."

Rascal yipped.

"I'm hungry too."

Wren examined the shelf that contained dog food and treats. "There is only one bag of dog food here, and it's a fancy, expensive brand; all the rest is canned."

Wren scooped a cup of the fancy dog food into a dog bowl, and Rascal chowed down. She checked the refrigerator case and found bottles of water, packages of sliced ham and sliced Swiss cheese. After Wren poured a bottle of water into a dog water bowl for Rascal, she made a sandwich, opened a small bag of tortilla chips, and opened a bottle of water for herself. She sat on the floor near Rascal to eat. "I was hungry; this is a feast, isn't it?"

After they finished eating, Rascal whined.

Wren smiled. "You certainly deserve your after-supper treat; and I need dessert."

She opened a box of dog treats; Rascal sat, and Wren gave him a dog biscuit. She opened a package of cookies and ate two before she closed the package.

"I guess if we're going to be stranded somewhere after a storm, a campground store with shelves of treats and cookies is the best place to be. I'm sure Taliyah learned from her dad; Eugene Hawthorne might have been a smuggler, but he was a brilliant campground host."

Wren's phone rang, but she didn't recognize the number. She frowned. *It's the same area code as the campground.*

She hesitated then answered.

"It's Crystal; I was holding my breath because I didn't know if you'd answer. My phone died, so I've borrowed my neighbor's phone. I can't come get you for a while." Crystal lowered her voice. "I stepped outside real quick, so we can talk. Our neighbors are older folks, and he started having chest pains. Dave is taking him to the hospital because there aren't any ambulances available, so I'm stuck until he gets back. I could use their car, but I'm reluctant to leave our neighbor lady alone. Where are you? Are you okay?"

"Thanks to your keys, Rascal and I are in the office, so we're safe."

"The office? You mean it didn't blow down? That's a shocker. What about your van? Is it okay?"

"It was thrown against the restroom building and is a mangled mess."

"That's terrible. What about food?" Crystal asked.

"The campground store has dog food, and I made myself a sandwich with ham and cheese from the refrigerator case."

"That's good; I'm glad you had the keys, so you have a place to stay where you'll be out of the elements and away from the bugs. I don't think we'll get any more rain, but the mosquitos would make you miserable. We don't have electricity; do you?"

"No."

Crystal sighed. "We have a battery-powered radio; it may be several days before power is restored to the area because we're so remote. We can probably come get you in the morning; will you be okay? I hate that you're there alone; keep the door locked. If you hear a car, turn off any lights you're using and stay away from the windows. If someone breaks in, lock yourself in the bathroom."

"We'll be fine; we have food, water, and shelter, and for security, I have Rascal."

"I don't think any looters will be out before daylight, but be careful; maybe you could sleep in the bathroom," Crystal said. "I have to hang up; I don't want to run down the phone. Be safe."

"Thank you, we will."

After she hung up, Wren shook her head. "Crystal's worried about looters; she wants us to sleep in the bathroom, but I think the door is too flimsy. The storage room has a sturdy door. I wonder if there's a lock on the inside."

Wren checked the storage room. "This is really odd; there's a deadbolt that locks from the inside. This must have been Eugene's safe room in case of robbery. The more I learn about Eugene, the more I admire him."

Wren moved the duffel bag, computer bag, and backpack into the storage room and rearranged the contents on the storage shelves to make room for her two smaller bags. She unwrapped the oversized outside mat she had found on a lower shelf near other camping gear for sale; after she rolled out the mat on the floor, she spread the sleeping bag on top of it. "I need something over me; I'll grab a beach towel."

She admired her handiwork. "Not bad. I have my portable charger power bank in my computer bag to charge my phone; I'll find some batteries for my flashlight."

After she found the batteries, Wren carried the dog food, bowls, and Rascal's treats into the storage room. "So, what do we do now? I suppose I could write until my laptop dies, but I'm too wired to think. Let's take our bedtime break, and maybe I'll get inspired."

When they went outside, Rascal stayed close to Wren. "The stars are beautiful, aren't they, Rascal? I see so many more than I've ever seen in the sky. It's breathtaking, and there's plenty of light from the moon to see."

Rascal wandered toward the campsites, and Wren followed him.

Wren pointed with her light. "Do you see that? Is that the trailer?"

When they were closer to the tangle of metal, plastic, and glass, Wren sighed. "It's Taliyah's car. Let's walk around the restrooms to see if we can find the golfcart."

As they rounded the corner of the restroom building, Wren froze when she heard men's voices coming from the marina and quickly turned off her flashlight.

"Rascal, they sound like the same two to me," she whispered. She stayed still and listened. "They must argue about their cargo every delivery."

Wren watched where she stepped as she made her way to the boardwalk. Rascal whined.

"They won't see us as long as we're quiet," she whispered.

Rascal snorted.

When Wren and Rascal were close enough to understand what they were saying, Wren jumped as a phone rang.

"What's wrong with you? It's just my phone," Sticks hissed before he answered his phone.

Wren's eyes widened. *I hope he's talking to Fat Tony.*

She exhaled when Fat Tony strode away on the path he and Sticks had used to go to the warehouse on their last visit.

"Yeah, we're at the marina," Sticks said.

He nodded while he listened. "Well, the thing is..."

Stick's back stiffened. "No, I wasn't going to make any excuses; we can do it."

Fat Tony returned and fidgeted while Sticks was on the phone.

After Sticks disconnected, he said, "The boss said it's our lucky day; we're supposed to load up all the cargo including what's stored in the bait shop. When we reach the warehouse, we'll be picked up."

"What's lucky about any of that? The bait shop is a bunch of rubble; how are we supposed to find any boxes in a pile of junk? How are we going to get to the warehouse? There's a big trailer crashed across the path. Why are we being picked up? Where are we going?" Fat Tony paced.

"There's a trailer across the path? Are you exaggerating like always because you don't want to push the cart through the woods? The boss said we're supposed to take all the boxes to the warehouse, and you know what happens to people who go against the boss."

"I don't exaggerate; look for yourself if you don't believe me. Besides, I don't like last-minute changes." Fat Tony crossed his arms.

Wren nodded. *I agree with Fat Tony.*

"You better not let on that you don't trust the boss," Sticks said.

Wren watched as they stared at their cargo. *Trust but verify.*

"Maybe I got lost in the swamp," Fat Tony said.

"It would have to be both of us; I can't haul this by myself," Sticks growled.

The two of them continued to stare at the cargo in silence.

"Maybe you're right; maybe we got lost in the swamp. If we drop these boxes off the marina dock, they'll sink in the muck and never be found," Sticks said. "It won't take long."

They stood on opposite sides of the dock as each man dumped boxes into the water one at a time and watched them sink. When Sticks was down to his last box, he glanced at Fat Tony's back, sliced open the box, and stuffed packets into his backpack; while Sticks was busy, Fat Tony quickly removed packets from his opened box, then dropped the box into the water.

When the two men turned toward each other, Sticks said, "Let's go to the campground; maybe there's a car or something there; if not, we can walk along the road to catch a ride to Tallahassee, or maybe we'll come across a car."

"What about the boat?" Fat Tony asked.

"We can't use it to leave the marina; did you already forget we're supposed to be lost in the swamp? I'm going. Do what you want; it doesn't matter to me."

"I'm going too; you don't have to get so mad about everything."

"Go!" Captain X roared.

Wren moved as quickly and quietly as she could; Rascal stayed alongside her.

When they went into the office, Wren locked the front door behind them. After they were in the storage room, she turned off her phone and locked the deadbolt.

"When we went past the restroom building, Rascal, I thought I saw something in the woods," Wren whispered. "We can check it later."

It wasn't long before she heard the men arguing as they neared the restrooms.

"I don't think you sank your boxes good enough," Sticks said. "You were tossing them left and right on top of each other."

"I took my time and took two steps before I dropped a box and waited to watch it sink. You shoulda said something if I wasn't doing it to suit you."

"What's done is done. How many packets did you grab?" Sticks asked.

"Two, maybe three; what about you?" Fat Tony asked.

"About the same," Sticks chuckled.

"Criminy, this place got hit bad."

"Better them than us; we'd be at the bottom of the Gulf. I don't see no cars or nothing; they musta evacuated."

"It's creepy, like everybody's dead or something," Fat Tony said.

"For a change, you might be right; let's get out of here."

"How long do you think it will be before the boss figures out we're lost in the swamp?"

"You better hope that's what the boss thinks; we gotta be long gone before we're missed," Sticks said.

"Where are we going?"

"After we reach Tallahassee, we're going our separate ways; that's the only way the boss will never find us."

"I don't like it; there's safety in numbers," Fat Tony said.

"Not in this case, bud. If you want to stand here and argue, go right ahead."

"Wait!" Fat Tony shouted. "I can't run that fast."

"I'm waiting just this one time; from now on, you better keep up," Sticks called out.

Wren exhaled. "They're gone, Rascal."

The tiny room reeked of stale rum. "They are, at that, lassie; but the boss will be looking for them before morning," Captain X said. "Get some rest; I'll take the watch."

Wren sighed then glanced at her phone and exhaled. "I have a text from Justin."

She read aloud, "Glad you're safe. See you soon. Love you."

She stared at her phone, then grumbled, "I didn't want a text; I wanted him to call me."

Rascal put his chin on her arm in sympathy.

"There's no reason I can't write until the laptop battery runs down. There aren't any windows in here, so the light won't be visible outside, and I can put the blanket against the bottom of the door..."

Wren frowned. "I just remembered I left my blanket and the wet clothes on the porch. They're practically a neon sign that someone is around and probably close to the office, if not in the office."

Wren unlocked the storage door then hurried to the front door, snatched up the blanket, and double-checked to be sure no clothes had escaped.

After she was inside the building and had locked the front door, she paused. *I wouldn't want anyone to take the envelope that Taliyah cherished so much.* She checked the drawer under the register and found a fat envelope in the back of the drawer under some papers. She stuck the envelope into her waistband then dragged her blanket and clothes to the storage closet.

After she turned the deadbolt, she leaned against the door and exhaled in relief. "My dad told me once that it isn't a mistake if it doesn't leave the building. This would have been a deadly mistake if I hadn't brought it into the building." Wren giggled; Rascal stared at her.

Wren sniffed. "Well, I thought it was funny. I've totally lost it, haven't I?"

Rascal grinned then licked her hand. She sat on her makeshift bed and rubbed his ears.

When her phone vibrated, Wren smiled. *Betsy.*

"I heard there was a big storm somewhere close to you. Did you get any rain? Are you in Mobile, or do you go there tomorrow?"

"We had rain and wind today; my plan is to go to Mobile tomorrow."

"When I heard about the big storm, I thought I'd wait to make your reservation for Monday night in the morning, so we could talk about how far you want to drive. Are you going to get away as early as you planned, or do you think it might be a little later?"

"It's hard to say; I'll let you know when I leave in the morning." Wren frowned. *How am I going to get to Mobile?*

"Perfect. So, what's up with Justin? I didn't see him today at all; do you suppose he's on a secret manhunt? I didn't ask anybody if they'd seen him in case he was leading a special task force except for a couple of people at the grocery store and the gas station. Nobody I talked to had seen him. I went by his house to ask him if he'd heard from you, and his truck was there, but he didn't answer the door. Somebody at the gas station said he probably went with Aaron to pick up Natalie's engagement ring in Tucson because he saw the two of them headed toward the highway early this morning, but that wouldn't have taken all day, would it? Nobody's supposed to know about Natalie's ring; I only told a couple people, but suddenly it seems like everybody knows," Betsy sighed. "I'll be glad when you're here; it's a lot of stress trying to keep track of Justin. Butch said it's not my job, but he doesn't understand. Is it late there?"

Wren blinked when she realized Betsy had asked her a question. "It's our bedtime; Rascal and I went outside for his late night walk and came inside just a few minutes ago."

"I'll talk to you tomorrow," Betsy said. "I'll let you know when Aaron gives Natalie her ring."

After Betsy hung up, Wren said, "I enjoy Betsy's phone calls and her wild assumptions; at least she takes my mind off my troubles except I just realized I don't have a plan for how we'll get to Mobile."

She rubbed her forehead. "I could talk to Crystal about renting a car. Maybe she could give us a ride somewhere that I could pick up one except I read once that dogs aren't allowed in rental cars; what do we do then?" Wren realized her breathing had quickened, and her voice was quivering. "I need to slow down; I've got plenty to deal with right now as it is." She exhaled.

Wren texted Justin. "Good night. Love you."

She plugged her phone into the portable charger and laid down on her sleeping bag with the beach towel over her.

Wren closed her eyes and rolled onto her side, but the hard floor hurt her hip; she rolled over to her stomach, but she couldn't get comfortable. She sat up, wrapped her knees with her arms, and put down her head.

"I'm too wound up, Rascal."

Rascal sat next to her, and she wrapped her arms around his neck and relaxed. After a few minutes, she laid down on her side and closed her eyes. Rascal stretched out next to her. Wren listened to his slow, soft breathing and unconsciously matched his rhythm.

Chapter Fourteen

Wren woke when Rascal whimpered in his sleep. She stroked his back and cooed, and he relaxed. She peeked at her phone. *It's four in the morning. Too early to get up.*

A light aroma of lime swirled around her.

"Time to be quiet, lassie. Wake dog and tell him," Captain X said.

Wren rubbed Rascal's shoulder. When his eyes opened, she whispered, "Captain X said we have to be quiet."

Rascal sat, and his ears perked up and twitched.

Wren listened; she heard the crunch of tires and the sound of an engine as a car approached the office then parked.

She heard a rattle from the front door then the sound of glass breaking that was followed by the creaking front door as it opened. Her eyes widened as she listened to the intruder open cabinet doors, slam them shut, jerk open drawers, and toss the contents then the drawers onto the floor.

Wow; sounds like a rampage.

When the trespasser threw open the breakroom door with a bang, Wren listened as the intruder tossed papers from the boxes to the floor then kicked a few boxes and stomped to the front door.

When the front door slammed shut, Captain X said, "You have what the thief was searching for, lassie."

The screen on Wren's phone flashed a text. Wren picked up her phone and read the text from Crystal. "Are you awake?"

Wren sent a quick reply.

Crystal immediately responded. "Dave's finally back; I'll leave in ten minutes."

"Captain X, Crystal's coming to the campground," Wren whispered.

"Stall her, lassie. Tell her to wait until daylight."

Wren sent a new text. "Rascal's still sleeping; we're fine. Wait until daylight."

Crystal replied, "Are you sure you're okay? Will bring fresh cinnamon rolls if Dave doesn't eat them all."

Wren bit her lip as she furrowed her brow. *I need to say something convincing.*

She sent a text. "Hide four! See you later."

Wren exhaled in relief at Crystal's reply. "Good plan."

"The thief is going to the marina but will be back soon," Captain X said.

"Is the thief the boss of the two smugglers?" Wren asked.

The lime aroma dissipated; the captain didn't reply.

Wren crossed her arms and snorted. *Why don't I ever get any answers to my perfectly reasonable questions?*

Wren furrowed her brow. *What do I have from the office that the thief wants?*

Wren listed what Taliyah had given her: the history Eugene Hawthorne had written, the letters between Eugene and Dorthea, old financial records, other old documents, and the envelope with notes from Nadia to Eugene.

Wren shoved the blanket and the clothes against the bottom of the door. "Let's start at the beginning."

She put the beach towel over her head then turned on her flashlight to go through the papers she had in her backpack. Wren carefully read each page and set aside the financial records that showed inconsistencies. She opened the envelope Taliyah had kept near the register.

Captain X hissed, "Lights out, lassie."

She quickly turned off the flashlight and turned off her phone while she listened intently for the intruder to return. She heard the front door creak and shuddered at the tiptoe sound of footsteps that traveled across the office to the breakroom.

"The thief is going through the papers again," Captain X said.

After what seemed like hours, Wren heard the trespasser leave the breakroom; she held her breath until the car engine started up, and the car drove away.

"Is that it? Will the intruder be back?" Wren asked.

"Oh, yes, lassie; you need to discover what the thief has been looking for." Captain X disappeared.

Wren turned on her phone as she rose to open the storage room door. When she opened the door, the sunlight almost blinded her. She glanced at her phone and saw three recent texts and a missed call.

She moaned. "I missed a call from Justin."

She immediately called him, but it rolled over to voice mail before the first ring finished. A tear of disappointment slipped down her cheek. *His phone is turned off.*

Wren smiled at Justin's text. "Good morning, sweetheart. I'll catch you later."

She responded. "Sorry I missed your call. Love you."

The other two texts were from Crystal. The first one said that Dave had returned, and the second said Crystal would leave in ten minutes.

"Crystal will be here in about thirty minutes, Rascal. Let's take a photo of the van, then I'll call the Mobile RV dealership."

When she saw the overturned van against the building, Wren exhaled. "If Captain X hadn't told us to leave the van…"

Wren swallowed hard then snapped several photos before she called the Mobile, Alabama, RV Dealership.

When the receptionist answered, Wren told her about the storm, then emailed the photos.

"Honey, I'm so glad you were in a shelter; it must have been terrible for you, but what a blessing that you and Rascal weren't hurt," the receptionist said. "Give me one minute while I put you on hold; I'll download your photos then talk to my manager."

Wren sighed. "I'm probably getting the reputation of being hard on RVs."

When the receptionist returned, she asked, "Wren, we looked at your photos; it really was a horribly severe storm, wasn't it? Are you at the campground? Are you safe?"

"Yes, ma'am, we're safe at the campground." Wren smiled at Rascal.

"Good; we have a driver who will bring your truck to you, so you'll have transportation. It will be delivered around noon your time; give me a quick call if you're going to be at a different location."

"Really? I never thought...that's a wonderful surprise, thank you," Wren said.

The receptionist had a catch in her voice. "Yes, it is."

After she hung up, Wren sniffled. "I've been stressing about how we could find a rental car that allowed dogs, so we could get to Mobile to pick up the truck. It seemed like our best option, but our time has been so slammed I haven't researched rental cars. I can't believe it, Rascal; the receptionist at the RV dealership said they'll send a driver here with my truck." Wren headed around the building; Rascal followed her. "I was certain I saw something in the woods earlier. Let's check it out while we're here."

When Wren and Rascal reached the stand of trees, Wren laughed. "Can you believe it, Rascal? It's the golfcart. The roof's gone, and it's pretty beat up, but it looks like somebody just dropped it in between the trees. I've got the key. I'm going to see if it starts."

Wren climbed into the driver's seat and held her breath as she turned the key. When the golfcart purred, she giggled. "Good girl, golfcart."

She maneuvered the vehicle between the trees and drove it to the registration building. After she parked it where it couldn't be seen from the road or the campground, she and Rascal headed to the front of the building.

After they were inside, she asked, "Are you ready for breakfast?"

Rascal grinned as he wagged his tail. Wren measured a cup of dog food and set his bowl next to the storage room door.

While Rascal ate, Wren stood near the window to watch for Crystal. When he was finished, Wren carried his bowl back into the storage room.

"Until we know what's going on with the boss or the thief, I don't want to leave any signs that we're here."

Rascal went to the front door and whined. Wren opened the door, and he dashed outside. When Wren followed him, her eyes widened as he raced to the driveway and disappeared.

"Rascal!" she shouted then whistled. "Rascal!' Wren clapped her hands twice and waited for Rascal's responding bark that let her know he was on his way back.

When Rascal didn't respond, Wren grabbed her stick and headed toward the driveway. She stopped halfway to the road and called out, "Rascal!"

"What is wrong with him?" she mumbled as she turned around and headed back. Before she reached the registration office, she heard Rascal barking.

That's his help bark. Wren turned to rush to the road. *Stop. Take the golfcart.*

As Wren ran to the golfcart, she ignored the stabbing pain in her knee until she fell. She used her stick to stand up then half-hopped and half-ran to the golfcart; after she climbed into the golfcart, she sped up the driveway. When she reached the road, she called out, "Rascal!'

Rascal resumed barking; she turned right onto the road and sped toward him. After a half mile, she saw him in the middle of the road; he dashed to the right and disappeared behind a stand of Cabbage Palm trees. Wren stopped where Rascal had left the road and called out, "Rascal!"

Rascal responded with a bark; Wren made her way past the patch of prickly pear cactus to the palm trees and saw Rascal standing next to Jolie, who was lying in the sand.

Jolie whined when she saw Wren. "Poor girl," Wren cooed as she hurried to Jolie's side.

When Wren saw Jolie's matted coat and the sand spurs on the bottom of Jolie's paws, she crooned, "Such a sweet girl," and "pretty girl," as she carefully removed the sand spurs from one paw at a time.

After Wren was certain she had removed all the sand spurs, she rose and spoke in a soft voice. "Come on, girl; good girl, Jolie. Let's go."

Jolie rose to her feet and limped along as she followed Wren and Rascal who continued to encourage her. When they reached the road, Wren patted the passenger seat of the golf cart. Jolie put her front paws on the floorboard, and Wren lifted her hindquarters. When Jolie curled up on the floorboard, Wren said, "Good girl. Let's go back to the campground and get you some water."

Rascal led the way. Wren said, "We'll be there soon; we'll get you some water and food, and I'll call April."

After Wren stopped in front of the office, she checked Jolie's paws again and found more sand spurs and gently removed them.

"Sweet girl. Can you go inside now? We have a cozy spot you can rest."

After they were in the office, Wren poured water into a bowl for Jolie, who took delicate laps like an ancient woman sipping hot tea, then followed Wren into the storage closet, flopped down on the sleeping bag, and sighed.

Wren hand-fed Jolie some of the dog food as she stroked Jolie's neck. After Jolie ate a handful of food, she licked Wren's hand in thanks. Wren poured water into a bowl and carefully washed and dried Jolie's paws before she applied the animal antiseptic she carried in case Rascal had any injuries.

Wren called April. When the call didn't go through, Wren sent a text to April. "Jolie is with us at the campground. She's fine. Wren."

Jolie sighed then closed her eyes. Rascal lay down next to her while she napped.

Wren heard a car as it came down the driveway; after she partially closed the storage door, Wren limped to the window and held her breath.

She exhaled with relief when she saw Crystal.

Wren whispered, "It's Crystal, Rascal."

Wren went outside and waited on the porch while Crystal parked in front of the building then climbed out of her car.

"Where's Rascal?" Crystal had a tote bag and a thermos in her hand.

"He's inside with Jolie, a collie who was here over the weekend with April; they left yesterday morning before the storm. Rascal found her about a mile away from here. I sent April a text to let her know Jolie was with us, but I haven't heard from her yet."

"Will we disturb them if we go inside?" Crystal asked.

"No, Jolie is exhausted, and Rascal is hovering, but we might be more comfortable if we sit on the porch. There's really nowhere we could sit and enjoy our breakfast."

After they sat on the steps, Crystal pulled two coffee mugs out of the tote bag and poured coffee from the thermos. "Our neighbors have a gas stove, so we have egg sandwiches, cinnamon rolls, and coffee."

"Wow, actual food." Wren sipped her hot coffee. "I usually let my coffee cool before I drink it, but this is heavenly."

While they ate, Crystal said, "I thought you and Rascal would go back with me. Do you have plans?"

"The RV dealership in Mobile is delivering my truck to me, since I don't have any way to pick it up. My truck should be here around lunchtime."

"That is great news." Crystal furrowed her brow. "You'll have to take the driver back to Mobile, won't you? What about Jolie?"

"I don't know; I'm hoping I'll hear from April before the driver shows up." Wren sighed. "Seems like I'm going from one complication to another lately."

"What can I do to help?" Crystal asked.

"Do you know if the sheriff has returned to Sirens Beach?" Wren asked.

Crystal narrowed her eyes. "I don't believe so; why?"

"Just wondered." Wren took a big bite of her cinnamon roll.

Crystal glared at Wren while Wren casually finished her cinnamon roll.

Crystal poured more coffee into both of their cups. "Were you asking for personal or professional reasons?"

"I guess you could say a little of both; I tried to call him, but he must have his phone turned off because it went straight to voice mail."

Crystal turned to gaze at Wren. "Are you in any danger?"

Wren met Crystal's gaze and sighed. "Maybe I can get in touch with the deputy."

"Or maybe I could help, theoretically," Crystal growled.

Wren nodded. "After we finish eating, I'd appreciate your logistics opinion on some documents I have."

Crystal smiled. "Right, logistics, and you didn't call the sheriff, did you?"

"Theoretically, no."

After they ate, they went inside. Crystal stared at the disarray. "What happened in here? Did the storm do this?"

"No, somebody broke in. Rascal and I were in the storage room with the door locked, so I didn't see who it was. In spite of the way it looks, it was only one person. I don't think the intruder found what they were looking for though because they began tossing everything around before they left."

Wren showed Crystal the financial records and the letters between Eugene and Dorthea.

"Somebody was definitely skimming the marina's profits, and the letters have the handwriting," Crystal said.

"My theory is that it's Nadia."

"I can understand why you think Nadia is involved; do you know where she is?"

"No, but I feel like she's close." Wren told her about the two men and the warehouse.

"Sounds like smuggling, but what?" Crystal asked.

"I lifted a sample from the damaged box they left in the bait shop." Wren pulled out the packet from her backpack and handed it to Crystal.

Crystal stared at the packet in her hand; after she opened it, Crystal softly whistled as she exhaled. "I would have thought drugs; these are counterfeit hundred-dollar bills."

Rascal and Jolie came out of the storage room when Crystal whistled.

"Hey, Rascal," Crystal rubbed his face then waited while Jolie examined her.

"Jolie smells as bad as you do, Wren; you just aren't quite as muddy as she is. If you two are going to spend four or five hours in your truck with that poor driver, both of you need a shower." Crystal narrowed her eyes at Rascal. "Wouldn't hurt you either."

Wren snorted. "I don't disagree, but there's the matter of the yellow van blocking the women's restroom."

"You can use the men's restroom. It's not like I expect any men to show up that will want to use their restroom, but I'll guard the door." Crystal strode to the store shelves then returned with baby shampoo, hair conditioner for children, body wash, shampoo for Wren, and three beach towels. "Here are the basics; do you have clean clothes?"

"Yes, but will there be any water to take a shower?" Wren furrowed her brow.

"I actually know the answer thanks to my architect husband. Did you see the water tower right outside of town? The water to the restrooms is delivered courtesy of gravity, so there will be water until the water tower runs out."

Crystal strode to the restroom and turned on the faucet. When a steady stream of water ran into the sink, she turned it off. "Water tower is still in operation. What's your next objection?"

Wren shrugged. "I guess I've run out of excuses. I'll wash Rascal first, and you can dry him so he can show Jolie the shower is acceptable."

"Good; grab your clean clothes. While you wash Rascal, Jolie and I are going to snap photos of these documents and the counterfeit money and send the pics to other logistics people."

"Do you feel like walking, Jolie?" Wren asked.

Jolie yipped then walked to the door with Rascal at her side.

Crystal smiled. "Let's go."

Wren and Rascal went into the men's restroom. While Crystal and Jolie stood guard at the door, Wren set the water temperature, then quickly stripped down to her underwear.

When Taliyah's treasured envelope fell to the floor, Wren said, "I'd completely forgotten about that, Rascal. Crystal and I can look through it after all our showers."

Wren used the baby shampoo on Rascal then rinsed him. She laughed when he shook then took him to the door. Crystal was ready with a towel.

"I have no earthly idea why I thought I'd be able to keep my underwear dry." Wren smiled. "Come on, pretty girl; it's your turn."

Jolie tentatively followed Wren into the restroom and stepped back from the shower when Wren turned on the water.

"I think you'll like it, Jolie. After Crystal dries you with the towel, and I take my shower, I'll work on your tangles and remove any burrs." Wren smiled. "Good girl. You'll be happy when you're clean."

Jolie stepped into the shower and moaned as Wren massaged Jolie's muscles while Wren shampooed her. "Feels good, doesn't it, girl?"

Wren thoroughly rinsed Jolie before she applied the children's hair conditioner that smelled like watermelon. After Wren rinsed the conditioner, she jumped back while Jolie shook herself. "I learned my lesson from Rascal." Wren chuckled.

The two of them went to the door where Crystal waited with a second beach towel for Jolie. "Here's your towel, Wren; you don't have to come outside to dry," Crystal chortled.

"Ha, ha," Wren muttered as she removed her soaked underwear. When she stepped into the shower, she sighed as the water flowed over her aching muscles. "Jolie was right; this feels wonderful."

She washed with the soapy body wash then shampooed her hair. While she dried off with a clean towel, she smiled. "I'll bet I rivaled Captain X in the aroma department."

When she stepped out of the restroom with her dirty clothes and the bottles of shampoo, conditioner, and soap, she said, "The shower was unbelievable."

"Jolie loved her rubdown, didn't you, girl?" Crystal smiled when Jolie gave her hand a quick lick. "You all smell much better."

"I found something I forgot I had," Wren said as they strolled back to the office. "I'll show you later."

"Your eye is still black, but your abrasions are almost gone, and you aren't limping as much as you were yesterday. How are you feeling?" Crystal asked.

"Thanks to the shower, I feel amazing," Wren said.

After they were inside the office, Wren gave treats to Rascal and Jolie then refilled their water bowl.

Crystal found a detangler brush for long hair. "Do you think this will work for Jolie?"

"I'll try it; we'll see how it goes."

Wren gently brushed Jolie's matted hair and tangles, and Jolie leaned against her and closed her eyes.

When Wren put down the brush, Crystal stroked Jolie's back. "Your coat feels so silky; you're a pretty girl, Jolie."

After Wren flipped over her sleeping bag, Jolie circled it, then laid down; Rascal laid next to her while Wren applied more antiseptic to Jolie's paws.

When Wren left the storage room, she partially closed the door, so it would be dark enough for Jolie to nap.

Crystal's phone buzzed a text. "My logistics friends are asking if there are any more packets like this."

"They dumped most of their cargo today off the side of the dock at the marina and waited until the packets sank into the mud before they left. Each man took at least five packets out of their last boxes before they dropped the rest of the box's contents into the water. The boxes they had stored in the bait shop earlier were probably buried under the debris."

Crystal smiled. "That's great, especially the part where I don't have to be the one to recover the cargo from the water or dig through the rubble."

"I don't really know how long they leave the boxes in their warehouse," Wren said.

"I'd forgotten about the warehouse. Where is it exactly?" Crystal asked.

Wren pulled up a map of the campground on her phone then pointed at the roads. "Here's the campground, and here's the roadside park with the warehouse behind it."

Crystal raised an eyebrow. "Did you check it before the storm? Weren't you worried your big yellow van would be noticeable?"

"Exactly, which is why I borrowed Taliyah's car," Wren said.

Crystal burst out laughing. "You are a trip, Wren Weaver. Did you see anything?"

"The padlock was exactly like the one on the bait shop; it looked locked from the distance, but it wasn't. There were boxes stacked along the back wall, but that was all I saw because a truck turned at the roadside park, so I returned the padlock to its original position and went through the woods to Taliyah's car and left."

"Did you take a picture of the boxes inside the building?"

Wren checked her phone. "Yes, here it is. I didn't even look at it because it was so dark in the building."

Crystal shook her head. "You're right; it's dark, but it can be enhanced; send it to me. Did you see the truck? Did it have any markings?"

"The truck was a rental transport truck."

"Your observation skills are phenomenal; if you ever become bored with the tame world of journalism, I could use a good logistics partner."

Wren giggled. "So far, my career as a journalist has not been tame."

"I can't argue with that. I'm going to check out the roadside park. Will you be okay here?"

"We'll be fine. I'll lock the front door; if anyone shows up, Rascal, Jolie, and I will stay out of sight in the storage room."

"Text me if you need me." Crystal left.

Wren looked at her phone. "I only have one number for April. I wonder if Taliyah had a number for her husband."

Wren exhaled as she surveyed the papers scattered all over the floor. *I'd wreck my knee trying to pick up all these papers.*

She grabbed a broom and tried to sweep the papers into a corner, but the papers were flat on the floor and didn't budge; she glared at the litter on the floor then returned the broom to the corner where she'd found it.

Wren picked up a drawer; underneath it was a 6-inch by nine-inch wire bound notebook. The cover was alternating stripes of a pale olive green and cream with the Lost Pirate Campground logo in the middle of the notebook. Wren smiled at the pirate in the center of the logo. *Crystal should change the logo. Captain X would never wear a frilly shirt like that.*

Wren pulled away the elastic band of dark olive green that held the book closed and read the first page. *Taliyah kept a manual record of her guests.*

Wren frowned. *No, this looks more like Eugene's handwriting, and these aren't RV brands and models, they are boat manufacturers and boat names. What was he tracking?*

She turned page after page until she came to a note at the bottom of a page that was circled in red ink. "Overall annual shortfall, $1.5M."

Wow, that's definitely a significant amount of money for a shortage.

"More for the logistics crowd," Wren mumbled as she scanned the room for more bound notebooks but didn't see any.

"I wonder if Eugene was tracking shortages in the counterfeit money he was smuggling."

Chapter Fifteen

Wren stared at Taliyah's computer. *I wonder if she slid notes under her keyboard.* Wren lifted the keyboard and found scraps of paper.

She found one that said, "Charlie" with Charlie's phone number on it, and another with her name and her number. She found a slip that said "April" with two phone numbers.

Wren's phone flashed a text from Crystal. "I saw the building and took a peek inside; they must have seen my car because there's a truck blocking the exit. I think they're waiting for me. How do I find the path back to the marina?"

"It's parallel to the road then it takes a sharp right in about a half mile from the roadside park. Do you want us to meet you?"

"Not yet. Will let you know."

Wren took the pirate logo notebook with her to the storage room.

"Crystal is walking back from the warehouse to the marina, but Fat Tony said the path to the warehouse was blocked by something large, like a trailer; she can't return that way, can she, Rascal?"

Rascal whined.

Wren checked the satellite view of the map and focused on the brush and trees behind the campground. "I think I see another way."

She sent a text to Crystal. "When you're about a quarter mile from the warehouse, turn south."

A few minutes later, Crystal replied, "I should have worn a long-sleeved shirt."

Wren scrutinized the map. "Rascal, I think she must be going through an area that has palms with sharp leaves or thorns."

She sent Crystal a text: "Turn east until you are away from the spikey leaves then turn south."

Crystal replied, "Will do."

Jolie whined.

"Let's go outside and watch for Crystal; while you take a break, I have another number I can try for April."

Wren sat on the porch while Rascal and Jolie wandered around in front of the registration building. She called the second number, and her call rolled over to voice mail after six rings.

After Wren listened to the male voice who mentioned only the number she called but not a name, she said, "This is Wren; I'm calling to tell April that Jolie is at the campground with us."

Her phone rang. *It's the number I just called.*

"Wren, you really have Jolie?" April's voice was hoarse.

"Rascal found her about a mile away from the campground; she's fine. She had sand spurs in her paws and was exhausted.

After water, food, and a shower, she's feeling much better. She and Rascal are exploring the campground."

"Oh, my goodness; I can't believe she almost made it to the campground. You won't believe it, Wren. We saw the storm coming straight at us, so we turned back to try to outrun it. We couldn't find anywhere to shelter; when it was almost on top of us about ten miles from the campground, we jumped out of the truck and laid down in a ditch. Corky and I held onto each other with Jolie between us. I honestly thought the ditch would be our grave. When the storm finally passed us, Jolie was gone. Our truck and trailer were across the road in a field. A farmer and his son helped Corky get the truck out of the field, but the trailer has a broken axle. I can't believe Rascal found her. Was she barking?"

"No, Rascal and I went outside for a break, and he suddenly raced down the driveway. The campground golfcart was drivable, so I chased after him. When we found her near the road, I was glad I had the golfcart because she was completely exhausted."

"I'm so thankful you found her. We've been walking the fields and the roads and calling her..." April's voice cracked. "Corky and I thought we'd lost her; we'll be there in twenty minutes."

"We'll be inside the office," Wren said.

After she hung up, Wren turned toward the office building; Rascal and Jolie trotted to join her.

When they went inside, Jolie and Rascal drank their fill of water. Wren gave Jolie a half-portion of dog food; when Rascal stared at her, she put half of what she had given Jolie into a small bowl for him. After they ate, she gave both of them a treat.

When a beat-up truck pulled in front of the office, April climbed out of the passenger's seat and limped into the office. Her arms were scratched and bleeding. Jolie whined and hurried to April; April knelt down and hugged Jolie. "Thank you so much, Wren. I lost my phone during the storm. How did you get Corky's number?"

"I called and texted your number as soon as we found Jolie, but when you didn't return my call or my text, I searched for another number and found a note under the keyboard in the office; it had your name and two numbers."

April shook her head. "I am so grateful. I hate to hug and run, but our trailer will be towed in the next half hour. We want to follow the tow truck, so we'll know where our trailer is."

April hugged Rascal. "Thank you, Rascal; you're a genuine hero."

April hugged Wren and whispered, "Thank you so much."

After April and Jolie left, Wren said, "Can you believe we found April? Thank goodness Taliyah takes notes."

Wren stared at the floor. "I was trying to pick up all the sheets of paper to see if I could find anything useful, but Taliyah always used scraps of paper; she could have picked up the habit from her dad. I need to look in the envelope."

When she opened the envelope, scraps of paper drifted to the floor. "I called that one, didn't I, Rascal?"

She bent down to pick up the papers that had fallen out.

"Taliyah said the envelope included notes from Nadia." Wren pulled out the folded sheets of paper and smoothed them out.

"Wow." Wren stared at the first sheet of paper. "The language is scathing, but what's shocking is that Nadia's handwriting matches up with the handwriting in the notes that were supposed to be between Eugene and Dorthea. Rascal, either Nadia penned the Eugene and Dorthea letters or else someone is impersonating all three. I know it's not Taliyah, because this is nothing like her handwriting. I wonder if Eugene found out about the forged letters between him and Dorthea."

Before Wren could go through the rest of the papers, Rascal yipped. Wren shoved all the pieces of papers and the folded sheets back into the envelope.

"Is it Crystal?" she asked.

Rascal nosed the door; when Wren opened it, Rascal dashed outside and toward their campsite.

Wren scanned the area; Rascal stopped and tilted his head. Wren listened then she heard men shouting in the distance. While Rascal dashed toward the dog park, Wren rushed to the other side of the registration building and jumped into the golfcart. When she reached the dog park, Rascal waited for her at the end of the trees. When Wren heard crashing in the brush, she sped to join him. Crystal was on the ground with her foot tangled in a vine. Wren pulled away the vine from Crystal's foot.

"They saw me; they're hunting for me in the woods," Crystal gasped.

Wren half-dragged Crystal to the golfcart then sped back to the building while Rascal stood guard at the edge of the woods.

When Wren reached the office, she dropped off Crystal, then hid the golfcart in the woods behind the office; Rascal met her on the porch. After they were inside, Wren locked the front door.

Crystal held onto the registration desk for support as she caught her breath.

Wren grabbed Crystal's arm and pulled her into the storage closet. "Sit down before you fall down," Wren hissed.

When Rascal joined them, Wren locked the door.

"This place is deserted," a man shouted from the middle of the campground. "I told you she doubled back to her car."

"We gotta check," another man yelled from the dog park.

"Nobody's been here in a while," another man called out. "No footprints here at all. Only tracks I see was a wolf that went through here."

"Let's check her car and the road," the man at the dog park shouted.

After five minutes, Crystal exhaled. "I got turned around and almost ran into them." She rubbed Rascal's ears. "Thanks for being a wolf, Rascal."

Wren asked, "Are you hurt?"

"Just my ego; they blocked in my car the second I left it; it's like they were expecting...did you see any security cameras when you went there?"

"No; want to check? I snapped a picture of the exterior of the building right before I checked the inside."

Crystal scrutinized the building. "You're right; there aren't any security cameras, so they didn't know you'd been there. The building looks fairly new."

Crystal leaned back and exhaled. "You may have uncovered a territorial war between smugglers. When Eugene Hawthorne died, there was no impact on a larger, established smuggling organization. Someone, probably Nadia, must have kept up Eugene's minor operation without stepping on the toes of the larger organization, except this new building looks like the smaller local organization is expanding. Logistics has been closing in on the big boys; Eugene's successor thinks you're closing in on them. I think you've made both of the organizations nervous. I'll bet you a cookie each side thinks you're working for the other; you've stirred up a hornet's nest, my journalist friend." Crystal chuckled. "And I thank you, and so does the entire logistics team."

"So what do we do?"

"We get you out of here as soon as your truck shows up."

"With no follow-up story for the Lost Pirate Campground?" Wren asked.

"You can't write a follow-up story; it's all logistics, remember?"

"I have to have a follow up for the storm."

Crystal rose and stretched. "I get it; it takes the heat off logistics too. Call Dave for an after-action interview for your follow-up. I know you'll do a good job, and I appreciate it."

Wren turned on her phone flashlight and pulled out the envelope from Taliyah. "There might be some help here."

Wren handed Crystal the letters of complaints from Nadia to Eugene.

"This is the same handwriting as the letters between Eugene and Dorthea." Crystal continued scanning the letters.

"That's exactly what I think. Taliyah liked to use scraps of paper and envelopes to take notes. I think she learned that from Eugene."

While Wren flipped through the rest of the papers, an old newspaper article with a photo slipped out and landed on the floor. She picked it up and held her light on it.

"This is old. It's an article about the benevolence to the community of Eugene and Nadia Hawthorne." Wren squinted as she inspected the grainy photo. "Nadia looks like she could be the librarian's sister, Crystal."

Crystal peered at the article. "You mean the librarian in Sirens Beach? I don't think I've met her."

"I have." Wren examined the photo even closer. "Put fifteen years and twenty pounds on this old picture of Nadia, and you'd have Laura with a wig and fake tattoos on her arms. I thought the tattoos were a vanity thing, but they could help hide her age; her claim that she had lost thirty pounds would explain any sagging skin."

"Nadia is Laura, the librarian in Sirens Beach?" Crystal asked.

"I think so."

"That's another reason to get you away from here as fast as we can. Who else would know that?"

"Anybody who saw and still remembers this article, but since it's been so long ago that it was published, I wouldn't think it would be very many people." Wren frowned. "The long-term locals who frequent the library would have known Nadia and Eugene, but Laura has the distracting blue hair and the tattoos on her arms, and their eyesight isn't as keen as it once was."

"Seems gutsy; why wasn't Taliyah a risk?" Crystal asked.

"I'm pretty sure Taliyah never met Nadia. Taliyah told me she had never looked in the envelope; she just kept it because it was a memento of her dad."

Rascal whined.

"What is it?" Crystal asked.

Wren listened. "A vehicle is coming down the driveway."

Crystal hopped up and went to the door. "Stay right here."

Crystal rushed outside; Wren grabbed her stick then she and Rascal quickly dashed out of the storage room after Crystal closed the front door. Wren peered out. "I don't see Crystal."

Wren smelled rum and salty sea air. Captain X stood next to her.

"The navy will need your help, lassie, to stop the thief. You and dog are masters at stealth."

When the car appeared in the driveway, it turned toward the campsites instead of continuing to the office.

"Crystal must have gone to the campsites, so the driver wouldn't come to the office," Wren said. "Let's see who the thief is."

Wren and Rascal slipped outside and crept toward the driveway as the driver parked in the first row three sites from where Crystal stooped to open an electrical outlet box. When Laura climbed out of her car, Crystal rose and smiled.

Wren and Rascal continued along the fourth row toward Crystal and Laura before they stopped parallel to the rear of Laura's car.

"You must be Crystal." Laura stood next to her car door.

"Yes, I am; how can I help you?" Crystal casually put her hands on her hips and leaned back to stretch her back as she shifted her feet.

Wren narrowed her eyes. *Crystal is in position to shoot.*

Laura strolled toward Crystal who had relaxed her left hand; Crystal's right hand remained at her waist.

Wren and Rascal crept along to stay in line with Laura, but out of her sight.

Crystal's gaze remained on Laura.

"How is Taliyah?" Laura asked.

"She's holding her own; is she a friend of yours?" Crystal asked.

Laura's chuckle was hollow. "You might say that; I've known her for years. I'm Laura, the librarian in Sirens Beach."

"Nice to meet you; I'll let the family know you stopped by to ask about Taliyah."

Laura took a step toward Crystal. "The campground looks deserted; where's Wren?"

"She left a few hours ago; Her boss hired a car to pick her up so she could go to her next assignment."

Laura nodded and continued toward Crystal at a slow and deliberate pace reminiscent of a bobcat tracking its prey.

When Laura was clear of her car, Wren's eyes widened when she saw Laura had a scarf draped over her right arm that Laura had rested across her waist; Wren pulled out her pistol from her holster.

"Are you taking over the campground?" Laura continued her slow pace toward Crystal.

Wren and Rascal silently shadowed Laura as they matched her steps and pace, but remained outside the range of her peripheral vision.

"I'll help out until the family hires an onsite manager," Crystal said.

When Laura stopped and raised her right arm, her scarf slid to the ground and exposed the gun in her hand. "I think I'll apply for that position; I'm tired of all the meddling from the family and that pesky so-called journalist they hired to spy on me and my operation."

"Now, Rascal," Wren hissed.

When Rascal snarled and growled as he raced toward Laura, he startled her and threw off her aim; Laura's wild shot grazed Crystal's arm.

Laura screamed and turned as she aimed at Rascal who had abruptly darted toward the rear of the car. Crystal flinched then regained her balance.

"You don't shoot my dog," Wren whispered as she and Crystal shot Laura, who dropped to the ground.

Crystal ran to Laura and kicked away Laura's gun then set her phone on the hood of the car while she called nine-one-one. Rascal rounded the car from the rear, stood near Laura's gun, and growled.

Crystal checked Laura then held pressure on her upper arm as she strode to Wren. "My shot was the kill shot; your shot was useless because you hit her in the middle of her forehead."

Wren's eyes widened. "That's pretty grim. Is that logistics humor?"

"I've never been shot before; I think it might be rage humor." Crystal sighed.

Rascal trotted to Wren and Crystal.

"Thanks, Rascal," Crystal said. "You're the best."

Crystal peered at Wren. "How are you doing?".

"I didn't reinjure my ankle or my knee or get another black eye."

Crystal's mouth quivered. "Not your norm, is it?"

Rascal leaned against Wren, and she hugged him. "I'm glad you're okay, boy."

Crystal tilted her head as she narrowed her eyes at Wren. "You were in so much danger here and rightfully suspicious of everyone. Why did you trust me?"

Wren shrugged. "That's easy. You liked Rascal, and he liked you."

Crystal gazed at Wren then nodded. "I'll leave it at that. Thanks for not disturbing my logistics career." She furrowed her brow. "Speaking of which, why don't you and Rascal wait for me in the storage room? I have some logistics buddies that will be showing up soon; everyone will be better off if you don't see them. I'll join you as soon as the area's clear; it won't be long."

"We can do that; I'll call Dave for the campground clean-up plans and schedule."

"That's a good idea, but you haven't seen me yet."

Wren rolled her eyes. "Got it."

After Wren and Rascal were in the office, she called Dave. "Dave, I need a follow-up for the Lost Pirate Campground to let the readers know when the campground will be ready for guests and the schedule for the improvements you already planned."

"I've been working on a new schedule; most of my rework was adding the building repairs from the storm into our original schedule. I'll send you my final draft; the owners are reviewing it, but I don't expect any substantive changes. It's fairly self-explanatory but call me if you have any questions. Thanks for everything, Wren."

Wren called Charlie.

"Are you ready for your next assignment, Wren?" Charlie answered the phone on the second ring.

Not hardly. Wren rolled her eyes. "No, I'm going to send you an update for the Lost Pirate Campground to address the repairs they're doing after the storm that raked this area. Look for it tomorrow sometime."

"I look forward to it." Charlie cleared his throat. "I called Carolina about Blake, and she called his mother. My sister said you won't have any more problems with Blake because she told him his allowance will be cut in half if he tries to contact you without her permission."

Wren snickered. "His allowance?"

"My nephew is smart enough not to cross his mother; she doesn't make idle threats."

And Charlie worked it so he wasn't the bad guy. Wren shook her head. "Blake would have been arrested if he tried to contact me, so you saved him some jail time and embarrassment."

Charlie chuckled. "I think that's exactly what your mother told my sister."

After they hung up, Wren checked the time. "It's only ten thirty, Rascal. I don't have to be anxious about my pickup arriving before I'm allowed out of the building. I certainly don't want to interfere with logistics."

Wren checked her laptop, but the battery had run down. She sent Dave a text. "Have the owners considered generators for the office and restrooms?"

Dave replied, "Good idea; I'll add them."

"I'm too wired to sit still, Rascal, and we're not allowed outside."

Rascal flopped down on the sleeping bag while Wren stuffed her blanket and laundry into a Lost Pirate Campground tote that was in a box on a shelf.

"I'm packed and ready to go when the driver gets here." Wren sighed then sat down next to Rascal and leaned against the shelves.

"Uncomfortable," she mumbled as she laid down on the sleeping bag.

An hour later, Wren jerked and opened her eyes at a tap on the storage room door.

"I can't believe you were so relaxed that you could catch a nap," Crystal said.

Wren stretched and blinked as she rose. "I think it was exhaustion and relief that put me out."

She stared at Crystal. "You're all patched up; love your new shirt."

"It ended up being a flesh wound; wouldn't have known it from all the blood, would you?" Crystal modeled her shirt. "I checked the boxes on the back shelves in case there were more packets; there weren't, but I found the Lost Pirate T-shirts." Crystal pointed to a Lost Pirate Campground gift sack. "There's one in there for you and one for Justin. I guessed at sizes; if I was wrong, let me know, and I'll send you correct sizes."

A tear slipped down Wren's cheek, and she hugged Crystal with one arm. "Thank you so much."

Rascal yipped and barked excitedly.

Crystal ran for the door; when she opened it, Rascal raced outside.

A strong aroma of rum and lime swirled around Wren. "You'll always be a pirate, lassie. It was a pleasure sailing with you."

Wren bowed her head in respect. "Thank you, Captain."

When Wren stepped outside, she exhaled. "My beautiful truck." Her mouth opened as she stared at the fifth wheel behind her truck.

"I'll be camping in a fifth wheel?"

Captain X roared with laughter. "That's not all, lassie."

Wren squealed and threw down her stick when the driver raced to her. "Justin!"

Justin grabbed her up and whirled her around while Rascal danced and yipped.

Crystal laughed.

As Wren's feet dangled, Justin snuggled his face into Wren's hair. "You smell good."

He set her down then took her face in his hands. "You are so beautiful." He leaned down and kissed her.

Wren pulled him closer for a passionate kiss that made their goodbye kiss in Arizona a mere peck on the cheek in comparison. When she finally released him, she gazed at his face while he beamed and reached down to scratch Rascal's ears.

"Did you have this in mind when you asked me how I felt about surprises?" Wren asked. "I never dreamed I'd see you so soon."

"Let me give you a tour of the fifth wheel." Justin's eyes twinkled.

While Justin opened the door and lowered the steps, Wren asked, "Is this a loaner or a rental?"

Justin motioned toward the steps. "Check it out; tell me what you think."

After Wren went up the steps, Rascal scrambled up behind her, then Justin bounded up the steps and opened a cabinet door.

"There are three slide-outs. Go ahead." He pointed to the toggle switches.

After Wren put out the slide-outs, she stared. "There's so much room."

"Let me show you how the sofa makes a bed." Justin opened up the trifold bed.

Wren laid down on it. "There's plenty of room for me."

Wren sat up and glared at Justin. "This is my bed, right?"

"Sweetheart, I'll argue with you about that after we're in Dry Gulch."

Wren giggled. "Perfect; I look forward to it."

When she stood up, Wren hugged Justin. "You really are here."

Justin returned her hug. "Ready for the rest of your tour?"

He kept one arm around her as he pointed with the other. "Theater seats, dining table with two chairs, electric fireplace, and chef's kitchen, whatever that means."

Wren giggled. "A two-door refrigerator and freezer, a microwave, a three-burner stove top, and an oven; that's an absolutely luxurious kitchen, and it's inside. I love the farmhouse sink in the island, and there's lots of food prep room too. I can try out the new recipes I have."

"We can learn together." Justin smiled. "The upper level is the bathroom and the bedroom."

Wren went up the three steps and peeked into the bathroom; she squealed. "An actual flushing toilet."

Justin chuckled. "Only the best for my sweetie."

"You have no idea how wonderful this is." Wren stroked the back of the toilet, the sink, and the shower door. "I don't have to empty a canister, and I can wash my hands and take a shower without going outside."

Wren checked the bedroom. "It's an actual queen bed, not one of the RV short queens, so it's long enough for you, isn't it?"

"Sure is."

"This is our perfect camper; I love it." Wren hugged Justin.

Before they put the slide-outs back in, Crystal called out from the bottom of the stairs, "I brought out all your bags in case you're ready to load up."

"We'll let your bags ride on the bed, honey, then you can put your things away this evening," Justin said.

After Justin loaded Wren's duffle bag, backpack, computer bag, and tote into the fifth wheel, Wren brought the slide-outs in; Justin put the stairs in place before he closed and locked the door.

Crystal hugged Wren while Justin opened the truck door for Rascal. "Thanks again, Wren. You and Rascal have inspired an entire logistics team. We are poised to take down a major smuggling operation, thanks to you."

Wren climbed into the passenger seat and clicked her seatbelt.

"Stairs are up, utility cords are disconnected, and Wren's in." Justin smiled.

As they neared the road, Captain X saluted as he stood on the Lost Pirate Campground sign. Wren waved and Rascal yipped. When Justin returned Captain X's salute, Wren gaped at Justin, then giggled at Captain X's resounding laughter.

After the turn, Wren asked, "You saw Captain X?"

Justin shrugged. "Doesn't everybody?"

He chuckled when he looked at the astonishment on Wren's face. "Thomas told me to salute the sign when I left; now I understand why."

Wren grumbled, "Is this how it's going to be? Are you and Thomas always going to gang up on me to tease me?"

"Sounds like a plan."

Chapter Sixteen

As they continued on the road toward the interstate, Wren leaned back in her seat and sighed. "Do you know how surprised I was to see you and how happy I am that we're together?"

"Tell me."

"Very." Wren grinned.

Justin chortled. "You used up all your words in your articles, didn't you?"

"This has been my toughest assignment: the campground was deserted, I was afraid to trust anyone, and I kept getting hurt. But on the flip side, I have two close friends: April and Crystal, you showed up with a bathroom that has running water, and we're together. Tell me about the fifth wheel."

"The RV dealership manager called me and told me the CEO and your publisher wanted to do something for you and gave me the CEO's number. When I called him, the CEO asked me what type of camper you would like to travel to Arizona, and I told him about our dream fifth wheel. He said he never would have received the detailed feedback that you provided from any other source, and he wanted to offer us a remarkable deal on our dream fifth wheel. Your publisher added a generous bonus for you because you've completely revitalized his travel magazine. Your publisher and your mother are friends, right? Our folks got in on the deal, and the fifth wheel is ours."

"What? This is our fifth wheel? We don't have to give up the bathroom?"

Justin chuckled. "No, honey. We don't have to give up the bathroom."

"Wow; what an exciting day of surprises. You and a fifth wheel. Where are we staying tonight?"

"We'll stay in Mobile at the RV dealership campground, then you pick out the next place where we'll stay."

As they traveled on the interstate, Wren told Justin about Crystal, logistics, the counterfeit money, Laura, and all the help from Captain X.

"Nothing you can write about, is there?" Justin shook his head.

"Not at all, except for the inspiration for ideas while I'm writing my novels."

After an hour on the interstate, Justin asked, "Ready for lunch? There's a rest stop ahead."

"Sounds good."

Justin slowed as he took the ramp to the rest area. "The receptionist at the RV dealership gave me a list of items to buy for the camper, like sheets, blankets, towels, and kitchen and bathroom supplies, and a coffee maker, which I would have forgotten. I shopped this morning before I hooked up the fifth wheel as part of my orientation at the RV dealership. While I was at the grocery store, I picked up premade sandwiches at the deli for lunch; I think I bought enough food to get us back to Hidden Gulch. She said we shouldn't be surprised that we'd forgotten something, but we at least have the basics."

Justin parked in a generous RV parking slot, then Wren, Justin, and Rascal strolled to the pet walk. When they returned, they went inside the fifth wheel, and Wren put out the slide-out with the dining table, so they could relax and enjoy lunch.

When they were back on the road, Wren's phone rang; she wrinkled her nose. "It's Charlie."

Justin said, "I forgot the CEO said you'd hear from Charlie, but he didn't give me any details."

Wren answered the phone.

"Where are you?" Charlie asked.

"We're on the interstate on our way to Mobile."

"Good, then you have your fifth wheel. How is it?"

"It's amazing; it has an actual bathroom."

Charlie chuckled.

Wren narrowed her eyes. *He's got something up his sleeve.*

Charlie continued, "The CEO just bought a campground in Louisiana..."

Wren interrupted him. "No."

"I understand you've had a rough week, but you deserve a vacation. It's haunted, Wren. Talk it over with the marshal then call me back. If you'll do this for the CEO, I'll make it worth your time and triple your pay. Your readers will be delighted with a surprise article from you."

Charlie hung up.

"I can't believe it," Wren growled. "Charlie wants us to stop at a haunted campground in Louisiana that the CEO recently purchased; Charlie said the travel magazine readers will love a surprise article about another haunted campground."

Justin nodded as he checked his mirrors before he changed lanes to pass a slow-moving car. "That kind of explains why the CEO asked me if we had to rush back to Arizona and how much vacation I could take."

Wren raised an eyebrow. "How much vacation can you take?"

"I told him up to two weeks, but I have twelve weeks of accumulated vacation because I haven't taken any time off since I was hired."

"Twelve weeks of vacation? What were you saving it for?"

"I wasn't really saving it; I wasn't interested in taking a vacation by myself," Justin said.

"Wow, so we don't have to rush back?"

"No, we can go to a campground and spend a couple of days exploring, or we could take Rascal to a real dog park and just hang out at the campground."

"Just you, Rascal, and me taking a vacation? I'd love it. If the weather turned bad, we could pick up and go somewhere else," Wren said.

"Absolutely. What's the weather like in Louisiana? All I know is Arizona weather."

"Probably humid like Georgia."

"I'll bet it's green; that would be interesting because I'm used to the desert." Justin scanned their surroundings. "This is all interstate; fine for travel, but it's miles and miles of boring concrete."

"Louisiana would definitely be different for you."

"Maybe I'll see the ghost. The only ghost I've ever seen has been Thomas."

"Are we talking ourselves into it? Are we interested?" Wren asked. "It would be fun to explore a haunted campground with you."

"If we don't like it, we can leave," Justin said.

"I wouldn't want to let the CEO down, though."

"Your call, honey. Both of us deserve some time off, and being together sounds ideal to me; besides, driving straight back to Arizona on the interstate would be like another deadline for you, wouldn't it?"

"You're right; we need a vacation, so we can relax and enjoy getting to know each other better. I'll call Charlie."

Charlie answered on the first ring. "I've been holding my breath."

"Justin and I talked it over; we'll do it. I'd love to write another article for the readers; the CEO and you have been very generous."

"Thank you, Wren." Charlie cleared his throat.

Wren rolled her eyes. *Charlie's getting soft.*

"I'll send you the details I have and make your reservation for tomorrow." Charlie hung up.

Wren shook her head. "I hope I didn't make a mistake agreeing to another article."

"I don't think so, honey; I'm really looking forward to the three of us being together."

"What if we hate each other at the end of a week?"

"Won't happen." Justin snorted.

"That's true."

Wren peered at the road ahead and shivered with excitement.

An adventure together...

Next to read:

BONES IN THE BAYOU

WREN AND RASCAL COZY MYSTERY, BOOK 5

Wren, Justin, and Rascal leave Florida for her final writing assignment: a haunted campground in Louisiana.

Check BARRETT BOOK SHOP for BONES IN THE BAYOU and other Judith A. Barrett books to read!

Browse, shop, read, enjoy!

Subscribe and Save

Join the eNewsletter mailing list and become the first to know about book specials and read unpublished stories and exciting news!

Be a VIP Read!

judithabarrett.com/newsletter

BARRETT BOOK SHOP

barrettbookshop.com

Browse, shop, read, enjoy!

FIND all the Judith A. Barrett books and series in the Barrett Book Shop to discover your next book to read!

More About the Author

Judith A. Barrett, award-winning author, lives on a farm in Georgia with her husband, two dogs, and chickens. She writes series for her readers: thriller, mystery, post-apocalyptic science fiction, and cozy mystery novels. Stories with a twist: not your typical characters from not your typical author!

Her motto: *You keep reading; I'll keep writing!*

When she isn't writing, Judith is working on farm chores, hiking or camping with her husband and dogs, or rocking on her front porch while she watches the sunset.

Website: judithabarrett.com

VIP Readers: judithabarrett.com/newsletter

Exclusive Discounts and Sales: barrettbookshop.com

Not into emails, even though Judith's story-focused newsletters are interesting, Not-Your-Typical newsletters? Follow Judith on Barrett Book Shop, Her Blog: The Latest Twist, Bookbub, or your favorite bookseller for news of her latest release!

www.ingramcontent.com/pod-product-compliance
Lightning Source LLC
Chambersburg PA
CBHW070221030726
47505CB00006B/1771